Being Forgot

Katharine Ann Angel

Illustrations
Robert Oliver

Foreword
Jason Gardner

2QT Limited (Publishing)

First edition published 2011
2QT Limited (Publishing)
Burton In Kendal
Cumbria LA6 1NJ
www.2qt.co.uk

1st Edition

Cover design & typesetting by Dale Rennard
Illustrations by Robert Oliver

Printed in Great Britain by
Lightning Source

A CIP catalogue record for this book is available
from the British Library

ISBN 978-1-908098-45-0

To
Susanna, Kirsty-Jane and Charis

*For sharing your parents and your home
with huge generosity and love for others.*

Reviews

I greatly enjoyed reading the stories! Each one was fascinating, absorbing and imaginatively written. Having read them all I'm sure the best policy was to read each with a bit of a break between because they are so thought-provoking, leading to much reflection at the end. Each stands on its own, though together they make up a superb social commentary. They are all suitable for KS3 and KS4 PSHE as well as for KS4 English Literature. Each story offers stimulus for group discussions, with scope for extension work. Several sections provide the teacher with the chance to explore beyond a PSHE brief as the stories introduce a higher level of knowledge, for example the war poets, GM crops, DNA testing, God, the planets and so on.

I enjoyed the style of writing, the jokes and humour, the topicality and the teenage contexts into which each story is set. The use of language and correct grammar are of high calibre and thankfully, Katharine has not been tempted to dumb-down either of them. She has dealt with some very serious teenage issues, yet successfully resisted the temptation to use shock tactics such as crude language to gain the reader's attention. Most teachers, parents, and students would applaud that. These stories are light-hearted and fun, without diminishing the significance of the topics.

Julian Lailey
Headteacher Ripley St Thomas' School Lancaster 1991- 2006

'Being Forgotten' is an impressive collection of stories based on Katharine's immense experience and intuition. This is set to become an invaluable asset for teachers and youth workers alike. The themes could be effectively used as part of an inset day as well as on-going training for teacher trainers.

Katharine's voice has a lovely turn of phrase, reminding me very much of Mark Haddon (The Curious Incident of the Dog in Night Time). Her brilliant use of language is so enjoyable: for example she describes a child's mother "tossing incomprehensible clichés along with the salad!" and another child burdened with "the trinity of grief, loneliness and rage."

Katharine gets into the individual mind of the child and echoes the child's voice with clarity and depth of feeling.

In my work as a tutor to trainee teachers, it is challenging to find creative ways in which to confront their misconceptions of children who are 'difficult.' Many children face huge obstacles that affect their learning and this collection will help our trainees empathise, by offering a vivid insight into the lives of some of their pupils.

'Oby' will be a very useful resource for my dyslexia classes!

Lorraine Partington
Partnership Development Officer, Edge Hill University

I am extremely impressed with these short stories. Katharine Angel lends a voice to youngsters who frequently find themselves ignored and misunderstood. Young people deserve to be heard and we would do well to listen and make renewed attempts to address their feelings of isolation and despair. This book will have enormous appeal to adults and young people themselves, and provide important insights into the lives of vulnerable young people. I cannot recommend this work too highly.

Tim Walker
Chief Executive The National Teaching & Advisory Service

This collection of short stories is a great way to introduce a number of topics that teenagers are dealing with on a daily basis. I will use them to promote a range of speaking and listening activities that will allow pupils to explore characters and emotions. The stories are short enough to be read as a whole class and will engage a wide range of pupils.

Cath Knight
Secondary School English Teacher, Archbishop Temple C of E Technology and Humanities College

Each story goes right to the core of an issue which is highly relevant to today's teenagers. Together they form an excellent insight into the different worlds of the troubled teen. As educational practitioners, in an environment of meeting attainment targets, the individual needs of students can get overlooked. The insights outlined here make a valuable tool for guiding and supporting NQT's (newly qualified teachers) and PGCE students. They serve well as a basis for thought-provoking discussion in PSHE classes for the 16 – 18 age group.

I used the story of Esau with a Year 13 group and it certainly sparked off an interesting discussion. The suggested topics (at the back of the book) gave them a start and they went off in many directions from there. The book is very useful early in the academic year, as new groups are formed, in highlighting to the students that they have a responsibility to include all members of the group. A range of stimulus material can easily be drawn from every story to suit a number of broader topics.

Linda McGuinness
Head of department: sixth form college with responsibility for mentoring PGCE students and NQTs. Personal tutor and teacher of PSHE to many 16 – 19 yr olds.

Contents

Acknowledgements

To my encourager: my husband Andrew. Your emotional reaction to reading Diamondman and Oby spurred me on to get these stories published.

To Susanna, Kirsty and Charis: for helping proof the text and enthusiastically encouraging me to keep writing! It goes without saying (but hey, let's say it anyway) that you are all beautiful, brilliant and the best a mum could get.

Talking of mums, Jean-Ann, we all agree you're simply the best. And to my very intelligent dad Robert (d.1977) who was proud of me because a teacher once wrote on my school report, "Katharine is always kind." On that same report I got a D for history but dad said, "It is better to be kind than to get a good grade."

To the children and young adults that I have been privileged to meet, teach or foster, especially the ones who inspired these stories; you are all wonderful and it was all worth the effort!

To Bob Oliver who agreed to illustrate this book in return for a kindness. May a thousand kindnesses be yours.

To Jason and Rachel: You have done so much to encourage young people to choose the best paths for their lives. What an inspiration to us all!

To Julian Lailey: one of the best head teachers I ever worked for. You knew the names of over 1000 pupils and nearly 100 staff all at once! Thank you for reading this manuscript and for loving Oby best.

To all of you who took the time to read Being Forgotten: I asked you for help because I value your opinions as adults who understand modern youth. I am so grateful for your invaluable reviews.

To Dave, Tracey and Bhupinder: thank you for your helpful memories.

To all my colleagues and friends who work with young people in and out of school, for those who work with young offenders, those who care for their families, those who run care homes or foster homes and in honour of our social services (I don't know how you do what you do but never give up!) and last but not least, to all you tireless volunteers who lead our various church youth groups and give so much time and energy year after year:

A MASSIVE THANK YOU FOR PUTTING
THE YOUNG PEOPLE FIRST!

A Foreword to
Being Forgotten

Numbers never give the full picture. It's easy to quote statistics when it comes to youth unemployment; the quantity of young people in care or excluded from school. And then there are the tables; schools competing for success or those large scale research projects that conclude with disturbing frequency that British young people are the unhappiest in Europe.

Titles and labels don't help the picture much. Take NEET (Not in Education, Employment or Training) or consider ASBO (Anti-Social Behaviour Order). Are these acronyms helpful? Are they even necessary? The jury's out. All the numbers, all the labels fail to paint the full picture, fail to help us understand the individual, the child behind the statistic and so we struggle to find solutions.

Stories, though, are different.

Stories help us travel into the heart-land; to get inside the thought life of an individual and their imagination. So even if it's only for the briefest of journeys you can step into someone else's shoes and see life through their eyes; then you begin to understand why they do what they do. Just for a few precious moments.

That's what Katharine has given us with these stories. Stories that are not spun out of the ether but are the result of having listened long and hard to people like Sean, Hetty and Oby - as a result of having lived life with them. And it's clear that as Katharine has sought to tutor young people, to help them cope with the demands life places on them, that the learning has been mutual.

For the past decade, my wife and I have worked with similar young people in North West London. We've been privileged to partner with youth workers and education and training initiatives across the UK whose motivation has not just been to hear the stories of young people like this but to transform them.

But listening to them comes first. It always comes first.

You'll find pain in these pages, inspiration, heartache and hope. Use these stories as tools to unlock people's understanding, to help them empathise with those whose life experience has been less privileged than theirs. Use them with students to help them articulate how they feel; to help them connect with their peers; to help them understand that they are not alone.

As I read, I found myself saying those two magic words 'if only.' If only things were different; if only they'd been given a different chance; if only we could do something.

Which of course we can; but first I hope that these snapshots inspire you to seek out your own Kirja, Pia, Rosa or Blake and really listen to them; to allow one or two of them into your lives, because there can be real hope for the next generation and their stories can have a different ending.

Jason Gardner
Youth worker in North London: Freelance consultant on
Faith and Generation issues
Author of "Mend the Gap: Can the Church Reconnect
the Generations?"

Esau

Being Forgotten

I was meant to be in school but no one noticed.

It was one of those days when nobody bothered to see what was really under their noses. In art we're doing Lowry and everyone in a Lowry painting is going somewhere pretty fast. Lowry paints stick people bending under the weight of the serious purpose of life, but I am not a stick and I don't fit into anyone's picture.

I am the boy who stands motionless while everyone goes around me with their noses to the ground. I am the fat boy who no one bothers to bully because I never react. I am the submissive one who steps quietly back to avoid a passing mongrel pulling on the lead of a reluctant man. I am the one knocked in the gut by that skinny woman, power-walking within her iPod world.

A blonde girl, excluded from my class last year, pushes a buggy over my size-nine scuffed shoes. She swears at me 'cos it's all my fault for being at the bus stop, for having feet that face forward across her path and she marches on in a cloud of weed and body odour.

High in the watery blue sky, white, woolly wisps unravel their jet plane trails, sketching noughts and crosses games that no one ever plays. I consider the

Invisible Ones seated in their tubes above the clouds, and it occurs to me that they will never know me. Their life continues as it will continue whether I, Esau Edwards, exist or not. No one above the clouds or on the earth below notices anyone else today because as usual, everyone is thinking only about themselves.

And so am I... thinking about myself, that is.

I stand at the bus stop with the usual crowd of pushing, bitching, smoking, swearing, pale-faced representatives of the parents of tomorrow. I am silent, the invisible one. Today, as usual, everyone piles onto the bus, rushing upstairs to claim the coveted back seats, except for me.

Today, I do not move. I clutch my oversized art folder and scraggy rucksack and observe as the driver of the bus nods, nods, nods, accepting bus passes as they flick under his nose, not bothering to recognise faces or to challenge the extra boy who'd slept over at his mate's and shouldn't be on board without paying. The driver glances in his wing-mirror as the door sucks shut, then pulls out into traffic without indicating. A mini-metro accelerates round the bus and cuts in sharply to avoid the central reservation. I witness this but I don't move. I simply stare at the back of the bus until I can no longer read the receding advert:

ALPHA COURSE
AT A CHURCH NEAR YOU.

Last month it was something about phoning the Samaritans.

It is possible that, in reality, I am not here alone on this pavement in Preston, on this planet in this universe.

After twenty minutes most of the rush hour traffic clears and the grumpy lollipop man outside King's Park Primary retreats with his metal STOP disc held high like a standard bearer at the end of a war. The battlefield is clearing. Right now I am 'Our Man in Bosnia,' the only truthful witness to the atrocities of life behind the doors of Fairstone Technology College; secretly filming for SKY news on a shrapnel-damaged mobile. This is Esau Edwards on location; Blackpool Road Bus Stop Preston.

The thought of my own unfortunate name triggers the playground voices in my mind: "I saw Esau sitting on a see-saw how many esses in that?" None. No S in that! I search for the letter S in my brain but it comes out as "S is for snake" and slithers away. I check my reflection in the bus-stop glass and I'm reassured that the boy I see is Me.

Myself.

I.

A skinny tree sprouts from its special place in the pavement and I kick lines into the dusty earth around it. I am a giant staring down to the midget world, squishing all the miniscule people into tiny blotches, merging their colours together and it looks like a Jackson Pollock and I am a famous no-hands-only-feet artist.

I am Wilfred Owen, war poet in "forever England on some corner of a forgotten street" or whatever he wrote… or was that Rupert Brooke? I can't remember who wrote what, so I rub my shoe violently over my unique dust design. I cannot draw, paint or even complete a painting-by-numbers before boredom sets in; etch-a-sketch was my artistic limit; up, along, down, back and squwirgle, which, if you ask me, is total talent and classy co-ordination, although no one ever said,

"Hey that's good, Esau Edwards, do one for me, do it again! Show me how!" No, no one even said, "Give me your picture Esau, let me see!" Anyway five years ago my ancient etch-a-sketch fell in the bath and I renamed it Wet-a-Sketch, then I chucked it in the bin.

Decision time.

Do I stay or do I go? While making the decision I trundle towards the traffic lights, my rucksack flung nonchalantly over one shoulder, because who cares that when I'm old I'll be in spinal injuries, having no-pain no-gain physio. Hey, I could win a Bafta for my natural impression of the Hunchback of Notre Dame...

"And the first prize goes to..." long pause ...hold breath ...raise an eyebrow ...envelope opens ...tense moment ...Nicole Kidman in a silver gown announces ...'Esau...Edwards!' The audience goes wild, cheering and leaping to their feet, crazy with excitement and I nearly fall off the kerb. Whilst collecting my incredibly heavy trophy I manage to negotiate a difficult zebra crossing and land safely and triumphantly on the other side.

I'm still signing autographs and resisting the amorous advances of Katie Holmes, telling her firmly,

"Go back to Tom, I have no need of your love!" when I arrive at the park; the park by the railway track, you know, the London to Glasgow line, the one grown-ups nag on about.

"Don't you dare go near it 'cos even though you might not worry about being killed by a train, you should be worried about getting caught on CCTV." They say that transport cops camouflage themselves as trees and leap out at trespassers and pull them along by their ears. Swings do nothing for me now that I'm thirteen, but I am still tempted by the roundabout. I turn one minute clockwise and same again anti-clockwise which spins the blood backwards to un-dizzy my brain. It's all to do with your inner ear. Not your left ear or your right ear or even your Starship Enterprise Final Front Ear. Ha, ha, an old joke I know, but you can't help thinking it every time! Inside your head, in the empty space between your ears you have an inner ear which helps you stand up straight, unless of course you whirl all the blood around in it so it sloshes about until you get vertigo and sometimes I do throw up.

I jump off the roundabout and stagger in the direction of the darkest corner of the park. Bushes and brambles arch over a muddy path, which slides steeply down an embankment to merge with a muddy track used by dog-walkers. Today is not the sort of day to feel afraid of the dark or strangers or being alone; in fact you'll never walk alone if you're a Liverpool fan, to whom I am totally loyal, except when Preston North End are doing well in the league. When that happens I say,

"Yeah, I support PNE and I'm proud of it. We're heading up to the top." Halfway through the year, Preston's magical winning streak is over and in my opinion they're heading for relegation so it's back to yelling "Come on Liverpool! You're invincible, untouchable!" I like to be on the winning side. Loyal to all but never a loser.

I think I am alone when I walk under the railway bridge. But I am not.

The bridge forms a shadowy arch about fifteen metres long and people are supposed to walk under this to the golf course on the other side, then along the bank of the stream for about a quarter of a mile until they meet the road. Then they either continue on to make a circuit home, or they double back on themselves to make the most of the countryside.

I walk under the bridge but I stop halfway and in the darkest space I look up at the dripping, greasy brick curve stuffed with ferns and moss. I make a small noise.

"PuP!" which echoes so I repeat my sound.

"PuP!"

Beneath my feet is a canvas of wet gravel and fag butts and blobs of dried gum, grey and white in the dim light and I think this is more like a Jackson Pollock and wonder about art awards and how I could easily make a quick fifty grand for this if I call it "Countryside Walk," so I frame it in my mind and introduce my masterpiece to the Tate Gallery and expect the usual accolade from the astounded adult world. This time, Nicole Kidman apologises.

"Sorry, I don't do art awards," she says.

"Hup-hem."

I jump. Reality strikes me with its light saber. No time to become Darth Vader. That cough is real. Glancing around, I can barely make out the slimy arch and the Jackson Pollock and of course, no one is standing behind me, ready to cosh me and steal my phone and bag.

Then I remember to look up more carefully, (because on CSI crime I learnt that people who search a room for clues often forget to check the ceiling or on top of the wardrobe) and I screw my eyes up searching for the tell-tale reflective eye of CCTV. I am trying to watch you watching me watching you.

"Ahem!"

That sound again. It's almost human.

"Ceugh yuk cooh!"

That's definitely someone gathering phlegm, then spitting it out. My heart races because I don't know whether to run forwards or backwards and my head whirls round like an owl looking for whatever or whoever it is. There's a movement in the shadows just where the arch meets the ground and suddenly a brick flies out onto my path. A crumpled monster is unfolding itself and snorting and the smell of drains wafts up from a mass of cardboard and rags. My eyes get used to the dim light and discern a black and orange sleeping bag which I recognise from the Argos catalogue because I once wanted one just like that. It's got Garfield on it, but this Garfield has been in a fight.

A small creature scuttles out from a hole in Garfield's eye where grey stuffing overflows like pus. Two more scurry out and I think maybe it's the three blind mice as a human body lurches upwards, and instinctively I step back because it must be the farmer's wife with a carving knife.

I bump my head on the roof, and it's a good thing it's almost dark 'cos my mouth is open but no sound comes out and I know I am about to meet the bride of Frankenstein.

The monster breathes heavily through its nose. Its long mane glistens in the shafts of sunlight that dare to squint into the space. I can see its eye! It is the grotesque Cyclops himself. The eye is reading me as it stares and stares, retrieving scraps of information from my incredible earthling brain before it disappears, whoomph, to planet Xeroxa to begin the human race in the fifty-ninth galaxy. I will be zombified, brainless as a baby, every cell sucked dry, never to move again.

"Ciggie?" whispers Cyclops huskily. What is it asking me for? I don't smoke.

"Er, no thanks. I..I've got a Lion bar," I squeak, thinking how brave of me to speak at all.

"Got a cigarette?" it rasps, though why it's asking for one when it's just offered me one is beyond my comprehension. I shake my head, wondering if it's male or female, young or old, alive or dead. It pushes aside a soggy wodge of cardboard and crawls on hands and knees out into the light. It is wearing torn grey cotton trousers under a baggy wool jumper of no colour, the sleeves of which hang right over its hands. It crawls and its sleeves go flip, flap, flop. I watch it slither away from me, face first, down the small bank to the edge of the stream and suddenly I realise that its feet are human, the soles are blackened leather and covered with scabs and blisters. It cups its hands and slurps at the clear water and I think how I wouldn't do that, drink from that river, it might have germs and there's a ton of rubbish upstream and rat piss that gives you Weil's disease.

The Body eases itself into a sitting position and shifts its feet forward, lowering them into the icy water and the whole earth sighs with relief. Finally the Body folds itself forwards dipping its head down between its knees and letting its face fall into the stream for about six seconds. Six-five-four-three-two-one, it hurls its head back, tossing its twisted, matted, brown locks, shaking water everywhere and the droplets sparkle in the sunlight. I'm amazed because when Cyclops the Body-monster turns to face me I see it is a woman with two eyes.

We look straight at each other and I don't know what to say, so I stammer, "I…I'm meant to be in school," but she doesn't reply. Her feet are still in the stream, so I ask "Is it cold?" and she says nothing. I think she feels nothing.

"Anyway, I'd better go," I add to fill the silence, then quickly turn round and walk back through the archway, just as the 9.15 train rattles and screams, cutting up the countryside nearby and I think, of a joke.

"What do you call a man with a train on his head? Coach."

Not even half funny.

"What do you call a man with a paper bag on his head? Russell."

Which reminds me of the bag in my rucksack stuffed with peanut butter sandwiches and crisps and a Lion bar, an apple and some fresh orange in a little carton and I thought what could I give Cyclops? Not the chocolate obviously because I always eat chocolate, but a sandwich and maybe the crisps, which are cheese and onion and not my favourite. I turn and the woman is crawling back to her hideout, the gap in the wall of the arch, and the arch forms a halo over the woman and I wonder how many people had already walked past her this morning and not known.

She stops as I approach and leans up on her elbows looking up at me with wide, empty eye sockets, like she's on the poster from Les Miserables. I rummage in my rucksack for my lunchbox and decide to give her both sandwiches as well as the crisps. I stretch out my arm while standing as far back from her body as possible. Our hands reached towards each other, slowly, slowly, the food crosses the chasm between us and I think about healthy eating and less sugar and five-a-day not just one apple. Suddenly, she snatches the food and our hands touch and it is electric, so I yank mine back quickly and hold it to my face, I don't know why, and it smells like a dog's ear from a dog with bad ears.

Then I say,

"You'd better have this orange juice. It's the real thing with vitamin C, I think." She croaks, "Thanks," and for no reason I am crying two tears, one from each eye. My red PE sweatshirt is crushed at the top of the rucksack so I grab it and toss it towards her. Then my legs turn towards school and I run and run and run.

*   *   *

When I finally arrive, wheezing, the bell is ringing and it's only break-time and no one asks, "Where've you been?" Later, Sir shouts at me for not having the full kit for orienteering and I don't know why Sir's bothered as it's a warm day and I at least have my aertex. He shouts and shouts, "Why didn't you-and-Where is your sweatshirt-and-you-will-get-a-letter-home…" until I open my mouth and explain matter-of-fact;

"I gave it to Cyclops," which makes everyone laugh, even Sir.

Oh yes, and later my mum shouts at me for muddy shoes to go and clean them now and stop crossing the school playing field in school shoes because at this time of year it's always muddy even when it's sunny because the drainage is bad in this clay soil. She can do so many words without a breath.

*   *   *

Every day, I stand at the bus stop and think about Cyclops and climb onto the bus, the last pupil, daring myself to miss it again, but I can't. So I attend lessons and I don't mind because there are so many things to dream about.

Then one day, during Monday maths, a prefect comes in to my form, carrying a plastic box overflowing with lost property and says can everyone check because otherwise it is going to charity and there is so much stuff with no name on. Behind the prefect is her mate, Shelley, with a bin bag full of named things and giggling, she chucks my red sweatshirt at me, with the label 'Esau Edwards.'

Sir yells, "Don't throw things Shelley! And Esau Edwards, it's time you learnt to take care of your property."

All the class shout,

"Oh, pooey! Stinky Esau! Do you wash your sweat-shirts in a toilet?" And I can smell cheese and onion crisps and a stinky dog's ear and it makes me feel sick straightaway. How did my shirt get to lost property I wonder?

My parents read the Evening Post and today it arrives with a photo of the railway bridge where Cyclops lives and the scouts cleaning up Lancashire for the good of nature and to save the planet. I read the article but all it says is, "Send in your photos of Lancashire's Grot Spots and we will judge the worst" and "Fly-tipper's cost the nation's tax-payer thousands." Nothing about Cyclops. They cleaned up the footpath and I feel glad no one discovered Cyclops.

But I am wrong.

My older sister who knows everything because she's studying performing arts at college and never misses an episode of Hollyoaks, leans over my shoulder and points at the photo of the bridge and says,

"That's where the old witch died," and I thought 'What do you know? She wasn't old and she wasn't a witch.'

"How did she die?" I ask. My sister screws her face up. She does that when she doesn't know an answer.

"What do you care?" she says and tosses back her wet hair.

I do care. I care a lot.

But I will never tell a soul.

Being Forgotten

Kirja

Scent of a Mother

It is June 9th and Johnny Depp leans nonchalantly against the wall, chewing gum. His benevolent, dark eyes follow Kirja as she dances lightly round the room, cheerfully putting her life in order. The sparkling collection of twenty-nine miniature perfume bottles stretches along the back of her dressing table, precisely three fingers width apart from smallest to largest, a line of delicate ballerinas reflected in the wide mirror.

Now Kirja stands on tiptoes, perching precariously upon her pink, padded stool, arranging her collection of fifty-seven beanie babies in order of preference, along the narrow ledge that forms a box above her curtains. First Kirja selects her favourite, an iridescent frog and remembers the order of merit until the last one is placed. It is a ridiculously floppy, pale-green pterodactyl.

CDs and DVDs are scattered over the floor, having been violently thrown against the wall by Hurricane Kirja. In time, the young girl collects up each one individually, as gently as she would lift a new born kitten. She scrutinises them with intensity, her petite face unsmiling, frowning as she discards those that are scratched or broken, while the survivors are replaced in their correct boxes and arranged in alphabetical order from bottom to top in the twin melamine towers. To raise her own spirits, the young girl plays music on her iPod, tunelessly singing lyrics she has repeated so often: "Oops, I did it again," followed by "I'm just a teenage dirt-bag baby!"

A further hour is spent polishing ledges, vacuuming the rug and brushing three fluffy, white cushions until, exhausted, Kirja swings round to face her admirer. She curtseys because to Kirja he is royalty.

"So?" she asks, twirling and sweeping her arm across her world, like it is a new creation, as perfect as the Garden of Eden before the fall. "What do you think?"

"Excellent!" Johnny nods as he steps down into the room and sits awkwardly on the bed, his gangly legs and pointed black shoes crossing and uncrossing. He leans backwards, then forwards, grinning widely. "But you need to ask your dad to get me a big armchair – or I'll always be messing up your bedspread." He lays his top hat carefully on her pillow and adds,

"I brought you some chocolate." Kirja pats her stomach and smiles,

"From your factory? That's mega, thanks, but I'd better not. Dad'll love it though." She touches the white bar to her face and shuts her eyes before inhaling deeply. The chocolate smells of Easter and caramel and feels like treasure because he has given it to her. Then she remembers something and opens her eyes, gabbling excitedly;

"Can I open it? Do you mind – even if I'm not going to eat it? Because there might be a Golden Ticket in it..." Johnny smiles, nodding with dreamy understanding, and he laughs.

"Hey, I don't own the chocolate factory young lady," he says, "That's Charlie as you well know. Why don't you wait 'til I've gone, so you'll have something to remember me by and I'll spin by tomorrow and find out if you won." Kirja agrees and places the chocolate into her locker drawer, next to yesterday's bar. Johnny rises, standing majestic and tall as the Pied Piper of Hamlyn and he twirls his long cane like a drummer in a band.

"You did a great job today," he smiles admiring the order she has created from chaos, and he adds, "I wonder what you'll be when you grow up?"

"Oh, I know, I know already," replies Kirja, tossing her long, newly streaked hair and catching a sideways glimpse of herself in the mirror; "I'm going to be called Vanessa and own a vineyard, just like yours!"

"Vanessa's Vineyard," Johnny laughs, his white polished teeth flash with approval, as if it is all Kirja's own idea.

"Happy Birthday, Birthday girl!" he says, almost hugging her, but hanging back respectfully, because after all she's only fourteen today and he is forty-five forever.

"Happy Birthday to you too!" she replies. Johnny moonwalks backwards, gliding smoothly to his usual position against the wall, strong and silent and dark and protective.

Kirja smoothes down the creases on her bedspread and moves Johnny's hat onto her locker. He always leaves it lying around, but one day someone will sit on it and then he'll be sorry. Everything feels right now. Sorted. Time to rest. Kirja lies flat on the floor face down and, using her elbows, she eases herself into the dark space beneath her bed, letting the bedspread fall back over her vanishing legs. There had never been monsters under Kirja's bed; from toddler to infant to junior days the space had always been warm as a womb, a place to sleep safe where not even Johnny could find her.

From across the street, the house looks shabby; paintwork, tiles, guttering, gate and garden all need attention, but it had not always been like this. Nowadays, it's enough of a struggle for Kirja to care for her dad and anyway, she's too young to notice when things are worn out or broken. She no longer expects a visit from her mum and Kirja accepts that she will be forever forgotten.

Since Kirja's dad's forklift truck accident four years ago, he has become belligerent, intolerant, demanding and her mum complained it was like having two children now and just because he's got no legs it doesn't mean he has permission to act so useless. *Just look at the Paralympics*, she screamed nose to nose with her man, because in her opinion the louder someone yells, the more clearly people get the point. She became increasingly frustrated because her life plans had never included a tea-towel in one hand and an iron in the other, a semi-incontinent, demanding husband downstairs and a moody daughter living upstairs in la-la land. Kirja's mum believes that no one changes the world by mooching around indoors feeling sorry for themselves; no, a person of value arms themself with a degree in history and votes against war, against tax, against school tests for seven year olds. You march against GM crops and American presidents and germs in hospitals and raising social security benefits. You pontificate against alcoholism and drug abuse and underage sex and overage sex and singleness and gayness and finally, your own marriage. Politics is the solution and if no one makes a stand, nothing improves.

Kirja remembers her mum tossing incomprehensible clichés along with her salad;

"If you always do what you've always done, then you'll always get what you've always got!" Then she would vanish for a day or two and who knows where? Kirja returned from school to hear the woman she called mum ranting in the kitchen about overcoming, equality for all, salmonella and the price of fuel. And they didn't even possess a car. Or eat fish for that matter.

Kirja can't remember the exact day her mum left for good, because she kept on leaving, each time for longer and longer, renting a flat somewhere classier than this dump, somewhere in London, for a week, a month, six months, until she stopped bothering to come home at all. Funnily enough, the last time Kirja set eyes on her mum was on Sky News.

"Kirja, come here!" Her dad had called her into the front room to watch the instant replay and he paused it at the part where the Prime Minister, head of Her Majesty's government, stands in a crowd with his mouth half open, half a word on his lips, hands clasped to avoid the commentators from reading accidental body language, and there is a woman in the crowd, frozen for a few seconds and it is absolutely certainly positive it really is her mum, alive and well and very thin. Kirja stares at the screen.

"Is that your mum do you think?" says her dad quietly. Kirja nods.

"Fetch me a beer," he says flatly and Kirja obeys immediately. That was the first night Kirja trashed her room.

Now her dad is sleeping soundly after his fifth lager and it's only half nine in the evening. Kirja's geography project lies muddled on the kitchen table, due in tomorrow, only ten per cent complete because the PC is useless and anyway Kirja doesn't understand the question. She scrambles three eggs together adding a little milk and marg and salt before microwaving it. She eats the lot straight from the bowl, then balances it on top of a pile of dirty mugs and plates in the sink. The phone rings and it's a woman from India promoting an exceptional offer for more TV channels plus broadband plus a phone-line. Kirja listens until she is a hundred per cent certain it is not her mum.

"Dad's out," says Kirja and hangs up. She collects two letters from the front hall mat and chucks them unopened into an overflowing recycling box under the stairs. She flicks on the TV and scrolls through every channel while her dad snores under a tartan picnic blanket. She selects a repeat of Grand Designs before retreating upstairs to her room, where she flops on top of her dishevelled bed and stares at the ceiling where a tiny spider spins a new thread and no one cares enough to toss it out of the window.

The trinity of grief and loneliness and rage wrestle inside her head, battle in her stomach, making her heart beat too fast, forcing the child to hold her breath and she imagines that her heart will stop completely. Suddenly she leaps up, gasping deeply and oxygen floods her body with a terrible exhilaration and she knows exactly what to do next.

Kirja's bed is Johnny's pirate ship tipping helplessly in the stormy waters and, without a lifeboat, the girl tumbles off it into a raging whirlpool. She yanks three drawers from her locker, raises each in turn above her head and throws them at the floor and with the mighty power of Zeus she sends lightning to strike the earth; she watches as marbles and plastic jewels and hairpins and jelly beans scatter like mercury over glass, into every crack in the floorboard, under the bed, the wardrobe and into the rug. She opens the wardrobe, flings clothes to the floor, crashes shoes against the wall, CDs hit every corner. Her beanie-baby collection showers down from the ledge, along with beads and buttons and pencils, homework and books and puzzles. When there is nothing more to throw, Kirja summons enough rage from within her tiny frame to wrench at her mattress and pull it to the floor. She tugs and hangs onto the baby-pink curtains until the pole relents and, like a broken mast, it crashes down among the flotsam and jetsam of a lost childhood.

Finally, Kirja rips from the wall a blu-tacked photo of herself sitting on her mother's lap and grasping a giant sunflower. Her dad took the snap on holiday in France six years ago. She rips it from the wall and using both thumb nails Kirja shreds it into tiny pieces, into fragments of feelings, now dead as broken glass. Each shard is a petal from a thirsty flower, and as she shreds, Kirja says, "She loves me, she loves me not, she loves me, she loves me not," until the yellow of the sunflower mingles with pieces of her mother's face upon the floor.

Kirja stands amidst the wreckage, heaving in a huge breath which fills her mouth and throat and stomach. The storm is over. In the quietness, Kirja senses the presence of a huge white dove flying overhead as mighty and gentle as a manta ray.

Stillness.

Stillness.

Kirja scans the scene and immediately decides to haul the mattress back onto the metal bed-frame before crawling under the bed and sleeping for six hours. By the time she awakes, the carer has come and gone, sorted out her dad downstairs and assumed that Kirja is at school. Kirja stretches, emerges from her chrysalis and puts everything right.

That was the first time Kirja trashed her room and the first time she arranged it into proper order by herself. Since then, the need to create physical chaos emerges with powerful regularity and Kirja cannot stop, even for food. After the sleep, everything she no longer wants or needs is placed into a cardboard box and everything else she arranges into immaculate order, wherever there is a shelf or a ledge.

When all is done she tiptoes into her mother's room, where her father never goes because, nowadays, he sleeps downstairs. She admires the beautiful collection of miniature perfume bottles from all over the world, touching each individually, as once her mother would have touched them, lightly caressing them with a single fingertip, absorbing into her soul the colours trapped within the glass, emerald and sapphire, golden and ruby. Rainbows and crystals and light and bubbles, mottled within a mineral so hard yet so fragile. Kirja unscrews the tiny caps, savouring each scent slowly leaving her favourite 'til last. It smells like white chocolate and she dabs it on her wrists.

Each bottle she moves, smallest first, across the landing to her own dressing table, cradling each precious memory in her cupped hands. The last bottle is the tallest, ten centimetres it stands so slender, with a twisted neck and a pearly stopper, shaped like a raindrop and imbued with the colours of a kingfisher. Kirja lowers it into its position at the extreme right of the mirror and as she does so, she catches Johnny's eyes reflected in the mirror, admiring her from the poster and he speaks not a word.

Johnny remembers her birthday because it's the same as his, but a different year of course. He reminds her that she used to have birthday cake and to check the kitchen for food and that it's okay to pretend Weetabix is a cake and that it's a real party with white bread and smooth peanut butter and four custard creams and a diet coke. Kirja skips downstairs. She pulls the washing out of the machine and strews it to dry across the kitchen chairs. One corner of her geography project pokes out from beneath a damp towel. Kirja peeps round the lounge door and the top of her dad's head is moving, and it looks like he's reading the paper so he is okay for now. Kirja creeps backwards and tiptoes upstairs unheard and unseen. Her world is at peace.

Johnny is waiting.

Sean

In My Own Words

I've got a lot more going on upstairs than you think.

Who I am is a fifteen year old male and my excuse for my poor character is my mum. And don't say I mustn't blame her, because you've never met her. What about my dad? What about him? Who's he when he's at home, which he never is? Come to think of it, who *is* he?

I've learnt how to handle the world by copying people fifteen years older than me who call me Thick, Stupid, Idiot, Liar, Thief, Moron, Lazy, No-Good, and YOU. These are not ordinary everyday naming words, but Proper Nouns, Pronouns; words used in place of my birth name and they all start with a capital letter. Those mature enough to verbalise them, prefix them with what I call vulgar adjectives, four-letter words that give these names deeper depth. More force. These are carelessly designed to create in me subservience, a big word meaning I'm supposed to serve under them; crawl at their feet; disappear. Thus I develop my inner fears and decrease self-worth. I could get them arrested for GFL, Grievous Filthy Language, or verbal assault, if I thought someone out there would believe me.

So what if I AM a Liar and an Idiot? I admit it. Look,

I'm raising both hands now; see my palms? Don't ask about the white scars on my arms. I surrender, it's a fair cop, I know who I am. But don't call me by the one name that gets inside my guts, because it makes me feel like punching your lights out. Oy! Look at me, because I'm only going to tell you once and its -

YOU

Hey You! Oy You! Over here You!

You, get here, now!

My head is a cavernous cave full of echoes, voices male and female, sounds in the shadows, coming at me from the left and the right, in front and behind me. I am jumpy and nervy, looking all round, wanting to obey before I'm hit, but how?

* * *

I was born on the bathroom floor, six weeks premature, miserably underweight and according to Mum I cried like a kitten, weak and high-pitched and I was so annoying even then. Mum still blames me for the nosey social workers, who were attracted to our flat, in and out busy as bees, collecting info and putting it in files for future reference, like there is a future for putting it right. It was also my fault when Split, mum's boyfriend, two-timed her when she fell pregnant then moved in with her ugly sister Maggs – oh, and while I'm about it, I'll explain how Split got his name.

Well, when he was in the infants he hung out with high school kids on the street every night, being proper educated in drugs and hot-wiring. Whenever the cops appeared on the Ruffey Green estate, the whole gang legged it like rats down alleyways, leaving little Split standing all alone on the park by a burning car. The cops left him alone because he was six but he looked younger. He could hear the big boys yelling "Split!" and he thought it was his name so he told everyone "I'm Split," and now he can't remember the one on his birth certificate. And the other thing about Split is that now he's twenty-six he's got rotten teeth and a terrible mouth stink, so when he yells at me his poisonous dragon breathe goes down my throat and you can't forget it. He left my mum but he still attacks me if we accidentally meet and reminds me that *he's not my dad* and he hasn't spawned any lazy effing morons.

I say nothing to Split, but it's the best thing in my life if he's not my real dad.

As I was saying, Split abandoned mum because she paid me too much attention, so she stopped sharing her vodka with him and Aunty Maggs and kept it all for herself.

Okay. So right now I can see a man in a black suit, standing across the hall, watching me. He reminds me of the undertaker at my cousin Darren's funeral. I can't help jiggling my leg and looking edgy because I can tell he doesn't trust me and it makes me want to leap up and grab his collar and ask him what's his problem. What does he think I'm going to do here, waiting for court, surrounded by suits and briefcases whizzing past my nose like I'm invisible? I'm on my best behaviour, hoping to get off a custodial sentence again, hoping to get moved from the care home to a resi. You know, residential: a school and a home and a youth offenders place all rolled into one. I want to go to Clifton House because, for good behaviour, you get a plasma screen in your room. And no, I'm not going to tell you what I did because you'd turn against me and want me locked away for a long time and the way that man is glaring makes me think he knows everything and he is my accuser.

The man and I lock eyes like animals, each testing who is superior, who is the hardest. I stare without blinking until that weakling blinks and looks away and I stop jiggling my leg and I chew my nails and think about cigarettes. A crying woman appears in the corridor and the weak man holds out both his arms and gives her a hug and they walk away like they love each other and they have nothing to do with me whatsoever.

I sit back in my metal-rimmed chair, leaning my head against the wall, arms folded, lanky legs stretched out across the corridor, liking my trainers, admiring my ankles without a tag for a change. They don't want me wearing it here. No tags in court. I am free 'til proven guilty. Important people are forced to divert around my feet and they scuttle by, hoping I can't read their fear of me and I pretend not to notice but I like the control. My body language mocks them, commanding them to go round or go through or jump over. You decide. No one jumps, but if they do I will coincidentally lift my leg at that exact moment and oops! Whoa! What a dive they will take. Imagine the commotion, what a rush! I can't help laughing out loud and so now everyone's looking at me and they think I'm high.

"Go round or jump over," I say.

Did you hear the one about the council workers who were painting double yellow lines along a road when they came across a single parked car? To save time and money they continued pushing their little machine all the way round the car, so later when the car drove off, there was a beautiful C shape on the road! And that's a true story about real people who got in the news for being stupid. They could've painted over the top of the car. Ha!

"YOU!"

That's my name. I look up and a large man in a tight navy pinstriped suit looks down. I raise my eyebrows as if to say, "Wha..?" which for some reason really annoys people.

"Sit up," he says "and get your legs in." Then he stalks off like a giraffe and I watch his back without moving my legs.

What is expected of me?

To be polite, intelligent, hard-working, (or to work at all), to have an idea of what I want to do next year, to go to school, to know how to make my bed, and to know what is real and what is fantasy. What *is* the difference between good and evil? How should I know? My tutor told me that kids can learn this from reading fairy tales, you know, wicked witches, princesses and junk like that. The first fairy tale I ever watched was called Silence of the Lambs when I was nine years old, at Uncle Rob's place. He isn't really my uncle, all the kids calls him that. Uncle Rob lets us kids do anything we want, help ourselves to the fridge, watch anything from his extensive DVD collection, and we didn't care that the food was out of date or the DVDs were terrible quality. Fortunately for you I can't tell you the story of Silence of the Lambs because I never watched it all the way from beginning to end; I fast-forwarded to the gory bits and rewound them about twenty times. Aunty Maggs said Rob is sick because he's also got loads of girls' films, like Sleeping Beauty and Beauty and the Beast and I've only recently twigged that they used to be books.

I don't know who to ask about some stuff in case I look stupid so I don't ask any questions that I should've known the answers to when I was six ...

like what is real out of Father Christmas, elves, Jesus Christ, pixies, leprechauns and fairies? I mean, they're all in books, aren't they, and I know people dress up as Father Christmas, but is there a real one, a central Santa somewhere? And why do people say God and Jesus when they have a good surprise on TV, like in 60 Minute Makeover, but then they say it when they are mad at me for bad stuff like breaking a mug or wetting the bed? And which is the one people pray to?

I have a tutor. She brings me real books, hardbacks too. I borrow the ones with less words, but I have to be careful I don't take anything if it looks like a baby could read it, so I don't get mocked. I've learnt all the big words about grammar from her and, don't laugh, but I like knowing stuff like adjectives and pronouns and extended vocabulary, I just don't let on to my mates or my mum. It's hard not to look as thick as a baby, at the same time as not sounding posh and brainy so my head gets messed up trying to act cool.

Anyway, back to my tutor and me. We meet at the Youth Offenders building where it's totally airless and the metal windows are painted shut. They give her a panic button, but she never has to use it because she calls me Sean and she believes I can pass at least two GCSEs: English and Preparation for Working Life. She has faith in me. I think.

The best thing is that I act so lazy that I have to have incentives!

Last week my incentive was Magnetix, which is a collection of ball-bearings and magnetic sticks and the power in those magnets is amazing! I made three-D shapes like quadrilaterals, pyramids and rhombuses by connecting magnet sticks to ball bearings. My shapes were strong and secure, because they had the most connected internal structure, but my tutor's shape collapsed in on itself as she only constructed it on the outside and the power of the magnets sucked together and the whole thing imploded into a right mess. She said that was like life and I agreed, because there's not much internal structure in my life, I just have to look cool on the outside. Right now I think I'm imploding, collapsing on the inside, trying to hold it all together. Also we designed magnetic cars and used the magnets to repel them across the table in a race and mine won by miles. It was brilliant...

If I lose this case I will also lose her as my tutor.

Here comes Jack. He's about fifty but looks sixty. He is my designated Youth Offender Worker and even though he is ancient, I pretend he is my dad. In fact, thinking about it just off the cuff, he could be my dad because there's no proof of who my real dad is. Imagine that! Jack *could* be my real father and I know how to find out for sure, because all you do is take Jack onto the Jeremy Kyle show and they will shout at you for being stupid and do a DNA test and I will try not to cry when Jeremy says Jack is one hundred per cent my dad and Jack will be amazed and say he always secretly knew it for years and that's why he's always been on my side. I will be amazed too, because my mum is only twenty-nine and much too young for him, so that's why I won't go on Jeremy Kyle, because it would make Jack into a paedo. Also, my mum would have to go on national TV and be shouted at for why I'm in care.

Also, I don't think Jack could fancy my mum, ever.

"Hi Sean," Jack sits down next to me and smiles, weary like someone who is tired of trying to get boys out of trouble.

"Only ten more minutes 'til you're on," I sit up without being told.

"I need a cigarette," I say, knowing it's best to wait in case I get called earlier than expected, and it will be any minute now because they're already two hours late. Jack has a smokers' voice that sounds like a cement mixer grinding gravel, and he used to be in the army, but he says he prefers doing what he does now, guiding boys like me. I know I'm not the only boy in his life but I pretend I am and, last Christmas, I accidentally called him dad out loud and the word just came up my throat and out of my mouth and it's the only time I've ever called anyone dad in my whole life. Jack pretended not to notice and just carried on as usual, but I thought about it so much all night that I nearly had a heart attack, then overslept in the morning and missed my tutorial.

Over the years, Jack says he's looked after two of my older brothers, one of my uncles and some of my cousins who live on the other side of town. My family is notorious - or maybe famous - and everyone has heard of us. Once *I* was in the local paper with my eyes blanked out, being called ASBO BOY and I couldn't be named because of my being underage, but I think it's because no one knew my real name and I don't know anyone who works on the Daily Post, so I can't tell them.

"It's time you stopped smoking young man," says Jack, "or you'll end up with a voice like mine." I look at his knuckles which are wrinkled as walnuts, which is a simile in case you don't know, and I stare at the back of his arms where his sleeves are pushed up and I admire his faded tattoo of a ship sailing through some long grey hairs. Jack once told me that he has his wife's name tattooed on his back but he won't say what her name is. Even Jack has his secrets, like where he lives and what he does after work, as if he doesn't trust me.

"So you *are* going to tell the truth," Jack reminds me, in case I forget why I'm here. He adds, "Were you just joking or did you mean to point it at him?"

"I told you it was only a replica," I reply, because they all believe it was a BB gun, something anyone can buy in a toy shop. I didn't tell them what it really was, because I chucked it down a drain and now it's rusting underground with the rats.

Problem is I stole it from my cousin Sarah's locker and her mates are waiting to jump me for it. I owe her big time so I'll need to find some money by next week. Sarah is the worst head-banger of all, but she gets away with everything by blaming it on her brothers and crying in front of the cops. She's got three babies and who would look after them if she got in trouble? That's how I know about Jeremy Kyle because she's always watching it and threatening her partners with going on it, so her kids never get to watch children's TV except when I babysit.

I took the gun when I was bored of watching the kids crawling around crying, getting on my nerves, so I nosed about the house opening all the drawers and cupboards. I took one of Sarah's tablets to try to get high but it must have been a pain-killer or something because it had no effect whatsoever. The gun was just lying in the drawer by Sarah's bed, not even wrapped up so I stuffed it down the back of my pants and went outside to look for a different babysitter. I saw Fat Mary on the street.

"Get here and help," I commanded, "You like babies don't you?" Mary's older than me and she can't talk properly so she never swears even though everyone takes the piss out of her so I think I made a responsible choice there. Mary just walked in off the street to watch the babies and she was dead happy and I just walked out feeling good that at least I'd left them with somebody.

Immediately after this, I thought of a way of getting the money I owed John-Peter Masters for nicking his weed and I never thought of the consequences, like Jack keeps warning me to do. Thinking of consequences is mega-difficult for me and if I wasted time thinking of what might happen if this or what might happen if that, then I'd never do anything and I'd drive myself nuts! That's how it happens with me, I have an idea and I do it.

Either I get caught or I don't. Mostly I don't.

So when two posh kids cycled passed me on bikes, I stuck my foot out and one fell off and got his leg tangled in the crossbar. The other, little cowardly brat-head, pedalled off like he'd seen Satan or Al Capone, so at first I tried to be polite and said, "Give me your bike," but the boy started crying and acting tough at the same time and he said,

"No, you...YOU!" The way he stammered "You... YOU" flicked a switch in my brain and I realised he didn't know my name, so I just lost it and pulled out the gun and held it right against his head and screamed at him in broad daylight to give me the bike. He went totally white and couldn't speak so I reminded him of what to do and I shot the gun at the pavement.

BANG! I nearly fell over backwards myself, but suddenly I had the bike and leapt onto it and pedalled like crazy down the street and that was it. I could've sold it to Springhead at the back of the bike shop and given the money to John-Peter but within ten minutes I got caught by a policewoman (a woman!) and I still can't work out how that happened.

A very thin female in a red suit stands right next to me. She lights up and blows rings towards me and I inhale her smoky air as hard as I can. An official comes over and stares at the woman and she drops the cigarette on the carpet and treads on it and looks at the man as if to say, What do I care? What you goin' to do about it? And she's right because he does nothing. The cigarette burns a black circle in the carpet and then I realise there are dozens of these circles all over the place like a disease. I look up at the woman because she's got a good body and high heels. She looks down at me and our minds meet. She feels sympathy for me like she understands and knows the feeling. I admire her for the sulky look and sassy attitude and I would've fancied her but she has thin lips surrounded by tight wrinkles after years of dragging on cigarettes, and weak hair, nicotine-yellow, yanked back in a pony-tail. Some birds make me sick. Jack glares at the woman, warning her with his eyes that say, "Don't talk to my client," so the woman speaks right into my face,

"Hello you." Anyone would think we'd met before, the way she spoke to me, saying YOU.

"Hi," I say, to annoy Jack and to pass some time.

"What you in here for?" she continues because she knows the score. She could be my granny but she still flirts with me. Jack coughs twice, but he can't really stop her; it's a free world and now I have to think of a story because obviously I'm not going to tell her the truth. I feel myself powerful, in control, invincible and ready to impress her with lies.

"Hey, you! You're next," interrupts the court jester.

"Here we go," I think and now that it's all about me, I react quickly, standing up, brushing myself down, ready for action. Jack is by my side, holding open the swing door for me. He announces to the room,

"This is Sean Sharples," and I smile because Jack is the dad I always dreamt of. He is a real man that calls me by my real name.

So I nod at the judge and I feel like a king.

Hetty

Who Cares?

Hetty believes in her own toughness. She doesn't believe in depending on teachers or parents or mates and so she misses school again; after all, she reckons no one cares. She slams the front door without a word of goodbye to her mother and heads out for what will be the most dangerous day of her young life.

More teenagers hang out on Shalloway Park on a Friday than during the weekend, but it's hard to see them, camouflaged as they are behind buildings and bushes. Today, two dozen pupils from years eight, nine and ten huddle behind the unattended sports' club changing rooms, acting cool, as they stuff their chewed and chopped school ties into sagging pockets. Their pale blue poly-cotton shirts hang loose outside regulation navy trousers. They share the cigarettes that they 'borrowed' from parents or scrounged from mates. Failing that, they inhale stale chemicals from pre-smoked stubs collected earlier from the gutters beneath the traffic lights. They share cans of Carlsberg, chilling out in the brotherhood of constantly licked cold sores, unwashed hands and neglected teeth.

Nearby, a dozen year elevens crouch beneath the bushes, attracted by the natural wigwam formed by overgrown hebes and rhododendrons, and this group feel superior for daring to bunk off GCSE revision classes, hardening their expressions into *who cares* and *what's the point?* They squat on damp rucksacks and stuffed PE bags, mumbling and texting and picking at leaves and twigs, or noses, nails and scabs. It's going to be another tedious day, hiding until three-thirty, waiting to drift home to lie to mum about how school was okay today, before collapsing wearily in front of chick flicks or computer war games, while faking homework.

As usual, Hetty is among them, languishing in the undergrowth.

Hetty is pretty but constantly weary. She combs her dyed-black hair with her chipped fingernails, fiddling with the gluey lumps that secure her tangled extensions. She re-applies makeup in the leafy shadows, using a tiny hand mirror with a flick-on light, scraping black eyeliner thick as charcoal, over and under her lashes, stroking ebony mascara upwards and downwards, ignoring the dark, dry flakes that fall onto her cheekbones. The makeup is easier to apply than maths and physics, which Hetty lost track of two years ago.

The boys remove their shoes to compare big toe nails. They progress to sniffing feet, feigning disgust and retching. Nauseated with hilarity, they compare tummy buttons, innies and outies, most filled with hairs and fluff and one stuck through with a silver bar adorned at each end with a stud. The skin around the silver bar glares red, threatening septicaemia, and the boy boasts that he inserted it himself, using ice-cubes and a darning needle and... oofff!

A soggy tennis ball lands in the bushes right in the centre of the gang. Seconds later, a muddy terrier flies into the space, focused only on his toy, flings himself at it, retrieves it and turns without stopping. He whizzes back out across the playing field towards an old man sporting a wide brimmed hat and brown mac. Automatically, the group sit up, rigid in breathless silence, as if to be discovered would mean certain execution. They peer through the branches at the younger kids, who are also motionless, pressed flat behind the wall, and the moments seem like minutes until Mr Brown-Mac and the hairy terrier exit through the park gates. A couple of ungainly rooks flop onto the grass by the swings and squabble over a scattering of last night's chips.

Hetty is restless. Her regular mates have bottled out of skiving, deciding to make a last ditch effort to pass a GCSE or two. Hetty wishes she'd done the same, but it's too late; deadlines for coursework have passed and warning letters sent home and messages of last chances to attend after-school tuition have been ignored. At least she hadn't been excluded like her best mate Sammy.

Mr Graham, the least inspiring geography teacher in the universe, lacked the charisma and skill to maintain classroom discipline. Sammy was not the only one to 'forget' her homework, but she was always the one Mr Graham picked on. Sammy complained that Mr Graham had the cheek to encourage her to sit on the front row because she refused to wear the glasses that she needed. Also, she added, the perv reported her to the headteacher for rolling her skirt up to well above her knees. So, only joking of course, Sammy poked her finger towards his sweaty forehead and accidentally touched it. Everyone laughed except Mr Graham, who lacked a sense of humour and reported her for assault. This resulted in two weeks' exclusion.

"Teachers've got no patience, and don't give us no respect neither. They have to earn our respect first," complain the gang.

"What're you going to do next year?" Smithy addresses everyone from his usual position, perched against the largest twisted root. He rolls on his socks and admires the holes created by his super-long toenails. Hetty listens, bored, as everyone rabbits on about college and shop-work, apprenticeships and a year out. Ideas of travel, leaving home, earning a million, winning the X-Factor; fantasies of the future tumble down amongst the dead leaves.

"What will *I* do?" thinks Hetty, but she has no idea so she says nothing, while picking at her thick, navy tights forcing the ladders in them to run down into her shoes. With a sigh, Hetty heaves herself up and crawls through the low branches, dragging her red bag which she has adorned with expert graffiti. She'd be a good artist, she thought, if she didn't have to think about chemistry and French.

No one asks her where she's off to, because they know she won't bother answering. The gang watch her saunter beyond the swings and towards the changing rooms, along the path which leads to the street. Suddenly, Hetty freezes. She overhears a woman's voice, authoritative, talking loudly to the year nines.

"What are your names?" she asks, but they are not afraid of the stranger, so they smirk like smart alecks and concoct names: Billy White and Lenny Henry and Kylie Smith. The woman is no fool. She recognises their uniform and speaks firmly;

"I will give you one chance to make your way to school. Now!"

This sounds quite threatening to Hetty as she eavesdrops from the corner of the building. The woman has her back to Hetty but her golden lab wanders free and smiles at Hetty with its huge brown eyes and wagging tail. A year nine boy from the group also spots Hetty and sticks a finger up in her direction so she ducks behind the wall, before the woman turns to check. The group acts cocksure, together against the single woman. Once again she commands the boy with the protruding finger to reveal his name, but he replies,

"I can't remember can I?"

The woman smiles, raising one eyebrow, sarcastic and unintimidated,

"That's why you need to go to school, young man, to learn your name." Hetty smirks to herself, as the little crowd lose interest in the debate and begin to wander towards the field exit. The woman continues loudly,

"I will walk my dog for twenty minutes. Then I'll go home and phone your school to tell them I have seen you. If you have reported yourselves in, then I will not tell them you were smoking, drinking and swearing. If you are not there, then they will be able to check who is missing on the register and I will tell them exactly what you've been up to."

The group slump dejected, like refugees with no command of the English language and no argument for why they are out of bounds. They amble off, weighed down with school bags and they wander, grumbling and mumbling, in the general direction of school.

Hetty backs into the doorway of the sports changing rooms, sucks in her stomach, and waits while the woman strides passed her, the lab eager to be off and running. After several minutes, Hetty leaves.

At the far end of the street she sees the group arguing about their next move. Hetty sits on a wall because she doesn't want to catch up with them. Those kids are so sluggish, messing about, when a green Volvo slows and halts next to them. The passenger window lowers and the driver shouts,

"Er... you really do need school! You don't know your geography! Turn right, not left." That irritating woman again. Her dog eyeballs Hetty through the rear window, still panting from its run, and Hetty reads a bumper sticker that says,

"There are three kinds of people, those who can count and those who can't."

Hetty doesn't get the sticker. Is it meant to be funny or clever or what? The woman drives home presumably to phone the school and wash her dog, while some of the kids head to school and the rest disperse to new hiding places.

Hetty walks towards town, conspicuous in school gear, inventing 'get out of jail free' stories in her head in case she is challenged by a community support officer: *I'm going to the dentist/I'm meeting my mother in town at the optician's / Yes officer, the school has given me permission. I'll be back there in an hour.* The main road is busy so Hetty repeatedly checks for the right moment to cross as she keeps walking. She also daydreams, and right now Hetty imagines that she is a famous artist with her own studio in London, with massive white walls and huge glass panes from floor to ceiling, casting natural light upon her own creations, the spray-can graffiti, multi-coloured canvases, textile bags adorned with chunky jewellery, magazine collages conveying youthful emotions, and incredible sculptures created from recycled metal.

"Bang!"

Hetty flies through the air, but she can't be flying, because someone is holding her arms and pulling her hair and pushing her down into a grey blanket. She smells plastic seat covers and hears throbbing unidentifiable music and a door slams. She is crushed and can hardly breathe and it is dark and darkening. She is face-down and trapped but she inhales and realises she is alive, in a car, speeding, swerving, rocking from side to side. She wriggles and tries to sit up but there's a weight, maybe a hand, pressing and squeezing on her neck. She kicks backwards, but her legs are bent sideways and she can't force them straight.

She remembers her mobile phone and panics because it is not in her hand and she can't tell if her bag is nearby. She hears a man talking and he sounds local, broad northern, laughing and telling someone to drive careful, don't drive like an idiot, you'll attract attention - and Hetty smells burning, like metal burning or rubber burning. She struggles and fights but hardly moves. All her strength is given to pushing up and twisting. A rough hand presses her face down and suddenly Hetty opens her mouth and bites hard onto the tip of a finger. Immediately Hetty feels a sharp pain in her ear as she is whacked on the side of her head and for a minute she drifts softly into unconscious, visualising her dad at work as a carpet salesman and her mum at Asda selecting the shampoo for dark hair that Hetty prefers and facial wipes that Hetty uses every night to remove her mascara and white bread because Hetty doesn't like brown.

*   *   *

The flash of a speed camera fascinates Hetty's brother, Simon, who is permanently excluded from school. He finds it funny when someone gets caught in the light and often amuses himself with this as he perches on the wall by the Texaco garage, scoffing sweets and smoking roll-ups with his new best mates, *The Excluded Ones* and it is not his fault that he has no idea his big sister is inside that speeding car, suffocating, so he burps on his Red Bull and his well-chewed chuddy shoots out of his mouth into the gutter. Everyone laughs. It is hilarious.

Hetty revives and is straightaway sick. The man holding her in the back seat is furious and bends his mouth close to her ear she can feel his breath swearing at her, telling her to behave so she won't get hurt. The sick burns her throat and she tries to move her face away from it. The man releases his hand and she sits up too quickly so she feels dizzy. Looking out of the window, Hetty is shocked because she is in the fast lane of the M6 and no one will ever find her. The men are laughing and the music thumps loud, and the sick smells terrible so they open the windows and Hetty wants to scream but there's no point and they know it. The air whooshes round the car, wild and freezing. In the front passenger seat a man grips the seat and bites his lips. His face is white with fear but he is feigning bravado. Hetty reads 'Sue' tattooed on his neck and the S of Sue is a red snake. He has self-inflicted tattoos – a letter of the alphabet on each of his knuckles; his right hand spells L O V E and the left one says H A T E.

Hetty is insecure without a seatbelt and twists to find it. The man in the back wraps his arm behind her back and helps her with it which adds to her nausea, because for that moment he is almost kind. Her bag is nowhere. Hetty looks out of the window hoping to attract attention, but the car she is in is travelling too fast, tail-gating the cars in front, flashing headlights, forcing them to swerve into the middle lane. Hetty's driver overtakes, undertakes, rarely brakes, until the man in the back says,

"Ease down mate. Next exit then second right off the roundabout."

Up ahead the traffic is stationary, backed up in all three lanes, hazard lights flashing red. A gantry warns, 'Accident Ahead, Slow Down,' but this vehicle does not slow down. It flies wildly onto the hard shoulder, ignoring the honks and shouts of other motorists and no one sees Hetty's face or reads her mind which cries, "Help!"

"There are three kinds of people, those who can read and those who can't, those who can read and those who can't, those who can read and those who can't." Hetty repeats these words trying to understand the meaning until suddenly she laughs aloud,

"*I can't count!*" The man next to her jerks his face at her,

"Hey, what's so funny?" Hetty blinks back to reality and she realises he is gripping her hand. She dare not move but now she has laughed a little and is grateful for being alive.

A very calm sound is in Hetty's head; a voice deep and calm and totally different. Only a single word, clear as a bell, near yet far away and the word is "Pray."

Hetty does not close her eyes but her mind and heart communicate with each other and words form, which seem to her strong and sensible and powerful.

"God, O God, God, O God." The words spill from her mind making her lips move and simultaneously she hears another word repeating,

"Womb. Womb. Womb." That is the sound of cars that Hetty is overtaking and the people cocooned inside them, oblivious and unknowing. Maybe it is true that only God knows. Hetty prays until she no longer hears the radio thumping, the men shouting and laughing, the engine roaring, and she loses the awareness of her captor's hand on hers and the sticky plastic seats and the rough blanket and she no longer smells the sweat of men or her own vomit.

The car spins sideways over and over down the embankment into a field and even though Hetty squeezes her eyes shut she can see blue lights. Then the world is black and there is nothing.

*   *   *

Hetty peers up into the eyes of a woman who is leaning over her. It's not her mother but Hetty recognises her from somewhere. On the white walls hang two watercolours of the Lake District hills. There is a chunky green sofa, upon which rests a large Paddington Bear dressed in a duffle coat and red wellies. Close to Hetty is a white, plastic table on which stands a glass of water and two digestive biscuits. The woman says,

"Hello, young lady. Do you remember me from the park this morning?" Hetty has no idea if she's in hospital or a police station or some sort of unit, but she is lying on a bed covered in a blanket. At last she speaks to the woman,

"What's your dog's called?" The woman says something but Hetty misses it. Then Hetty asks,

"What time is it?" and it only ten to three, so Hetty feels relieved because she'll be able to get home before her parents return from work. Another day and they don't need to know that Hetty missed school. No worries for them. No punishment for Hetty. She tries to sit up but a nurse is somewhere behind Hetty's head saying,

"Where are you off to young lady? Lie still. Relax. You might only have a few bruises but we still need to complete checks."

The woman with the dog explains that she's waiting to give a statement to the police, because she's a witness to Hetty's abduction and it was she who dialled 999 although it happened so fast that she couldn't catch the number plate, but the police had been brilliant, so quick, and they were there all the time following Hetty down the M6. They had to keep their distance waiting for the helicopter to be scrambled because they didn't want to exacerbate the situation and cause a pile up. The woman chatters nervously, reacting to the tension of the day. Hetty slowly turns her head on the pillow and sees a policewoman standing in the doorway, clutching Hetty's graffiti-school bag and mumbling to someone.

Suddenly Hetty's mum appears, rushing towards her daughter, crying and reaching out her arms and, hush! She doesn't need an explanation or an apology. Hetty hugs her, smearing mascara over her mum's white shirt, and no one mentions anything about missing school, so at that moment Hetty wants to be *at* school, to do well, to finish her art and try to pass English and maybe even maths.

The other woman sits, ashen-faced, on the green sofa. Hetty wants to say thank you but she is embarrassed so she says,

"Those boys, behind the changing rooms, they're not really called Bill and Lenny. They made it up…" and the woman chuckles because of course, she knew that all along. She isn't stupid.

Finally, Hetty's dad arrives, fretting and relieved and pale against the white wall. He kneels on the lino, and shuffles forward until his face touches the face of his beautiful daughter, whom he loves with all his heart and Hetty knows that she is loved.

Today she is safe and tomorrow is a new beginning.

Oby

Oby and the O

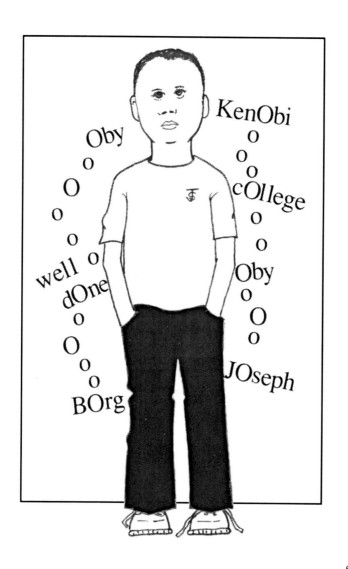

Oby stands outside the Head's office, rocking back and forth on his heels. He knows what's behind that door; every bluebird that flaps across the fussy wallpaper, how many birds face left from the floor to the ceiling; how many fly right towards the cabinet for the spoils of war, the trophies for music, sport and drama. Above the trophies, a royal blue caption proclaims, *Well Done St Joseph's Church of England Technology College.*

And there are five "Os" in that. Or maybe six.

Oby remembers that the letter O appears five times, one for each finger on his left hand, and he remembers that these round letters are five worm holes to infinity. Four holes lead to four universes, one of each for earth, air, fire and water, but the fifth one is the mouth of a tunnel that leads to death and destruction. The thought of the fifth O causes Oby to raise his left thumb,

"Five O" he whispers and his mouth opens like a fish without water. The problem, thinks Oby, is there's no way of telling which O is which. If he stares hard enough, one hole appears stronger, with a darker rim, like the O at the opticians.

The O in the word cOllege.

The optician asks Oby, "Which is darker, the left one... or the right?" as she changes the lenses quickly over his eyes. Oby doesn't know and he doesn't care so he says nothing. Nothing lasts forever, he reasons, not even eye tests or trouble at school, as long as you stand there and say whatever they want to hear, so Oby aims to feel calm until the test is over.

A bell rings and the Head appears, voice first, down the corridor. When the tall, suited man sees Oby, he raises his eyebrows, tuts and sighs loudly and Oby reads the Head's mind. The Head is thinking,

"*Obi-Wan Kenobi - we meet again.*" The Head doesn't speak but merely waves his hand with a dismissive, disdainful flick over Oby and marches straight into his office; so Oby stops rocking and waits.

After a minute, the door opens and the Head beckons Oby with his chin; *Get in here.* Oby obeys. Walks in, head down, acting sorry. There's a Toblerone-shaped box on the desk that spells *Mr P. Borg Head Teacher.* Oby focuses on the O in Borg, unsure if this particular worm hole leads to good or evil; while Mr Borg asks;

"Who am I?"

Oby resists raising his eyebrows. He resists making a thick sign by pushing his tongue over his bottom teeth and shoving it out against his lower lip. He thinks in his mind, *"Don't you even know that?"* However he says aloud from his mouth,

"You're the Head, sir."

Mr Borg stalks three paces across the room, adjusts his tie and rubs the place between his nose and top lip where his little black moustache would be if he were Hitler. Outside in the corridor some girls mess about, screaming and whispering and tittering. Oby watches Mr Borg tense up, his top lip thinning, sucking in air and grinding his top teeth onto the lower ones, like Oby's mongrel dog when it snarls. He half parks his bottom onto his superior leather office chair that twizzles while you work, but suddenly he changes his mind and rising like a suddenly erupting volcano, he turns to Oby, forehead to forehead, nose to nose, so close that Oby inhales his whisky breath. The whiff of whisky carries the raging flow of incomprehensible words up through Oby's nostrils, but Oby sees a high speed train whistle through a tunnel, the sound of its wheels on the tracks screeching as the brakes are applied.

"It's going to hit the buffers!" Oby's brain screams, as Mr Borg's tonsils waggle dangerously at the end of the track; and the engine is so loud – *"it's not my fault I can't hear what you're saying, sir, the noise of that train..."*

"...and your parents will be hearing from me, formally by letter and you will not return to the school for two weeks... and this is your last chance... Have you anything to say for yourself?"

The train is gone. Oby hears the last seven words and decides to say nothing, but his own little body disobeys and it forces a scrawny sound up through his throat. Oby hears himself protesting,

"I didn't do nuffin'."

Mr Borg acts surprised, raising both eyebrows, but he is apoplectic and his face turns blotchy red and white. He corrects Oby;

"I didn't do nothing, *Sir!*"

After two seconds Mr Borg corrects himself,

"I didn't do *anything*, Sir!"

Oby says; "No Sir. That's right Sir. Nuffin' Sir."

Mr Borg is confused, so he says,

"Double negative, boy. Didn't and nothing make a double negative, same as - did do something - so Ms Ferengi was correct to send you out of the class to see me. You cannot throw a chair at a teacher and call it nothing. You are a dangerous pupil and what you did is called in the criminal world, *ass - ault*. If the chair had hit Ms Ferengi, it would have been a matter for the police, nine, nine, nine, except that we cannot have police entering St Joseph's, think of the school's image – so be thankful that it's only your parents I'm involving." Mr Borg draws breath. He hesitates and his neck changes to blotchy orange as he adds,

"And they have already been phoned by me."

The phone rings. Mr Borg talks and talks while Oby listens, watching as sweat gathers in glimmering, oily patches across his greasy brow. Mr Borg says words like bloody and idiot and other professional vocabulary before he slams the phone down and stares at Oby because he forgot Oby is still in the room.

There's a knock at the door.

"In!" shouts Mr Borg, sharply. A small girl, year 3, pushes the door and her eyes and nose appear in the gap.

"Now what?" shouts Mr Borg. The girl is brave and speaks like a mouse on helium;

"Please sir. Sir, a lady is looking for you."

Mr Borg straightens his tie, wipes his forehead with the back of his suit sleeve, hastily ducks and peers at himself in the mirror that is hung four inches too low for him. He checks his teeth for chicken from his lunch and anything yellow. Runs his tongue over them. Satisfied, he pushes back his shoulders, stands taller, trying to be handsome and, turning to the mouse, he booms in a pompous tone,

"A lady to see me? Well, don't just stand there, let her in, girl." The door swings further into the room and the child scuttles away. A woman enters, tall and severe, her face pale as a ghost and her glasses slung low from a silver chain, resting on her chest. Oby is mesmerised by her sharp, pointy black shoes, a pair of shiny weapons menacing on the hard-wearing ribbed carpet. Immediately she glances at Oby and apologises;

"Oh, I'm sorry," she speaks and her voice is as smooth as crème caramel, but she is not addressing Oby, "am I interrupting anything?"

Mr Borg is not entirely sure who she is so he doesn't know how to play the scene. He asks a few questions and Oby listens to the strange grown-up world of language. His eyes widen in shock as the woman clearly says, *yes, I'm a spectre.*

Oby's heart beats so hard inside his rib cage; it is fighting to get out, get out, get out! His feet sink in quicksand and the spectre is blocking the doorway. Only his eyes move, flickering round the room assessing all possible escape routes. Window - closed. Air vent - too small. Roof hatch - none. The shoes of the spectre point straight at Mr Borg, but stay perfectly still and the voice of the spectre is luring Mr Borg to his death. Suddenly, she reaches out a long, blue-veined hand and touches Oby on his shoulder. His whole body freezes, even his brain, as if he has gulped down too much ice-cream too quickly. His eyes widen and widen until his heart stops altogether and he is a statue, petrified.

"Beam me up!" Oby shouts from his heart and immediately he sees six Os dancing before his eyes and all he has to do is choose the right one through which to escape and he will be safe.

dOne jOseph technOlOgy cOllege bOrg

The **O**s all jump out and there is no clue which is right because Oby cannot read. He cannot read and he cannot ask for help, because no one must know. He would rather throw a chair and be excluded than anyone should know that he is thick, stupid, idiot, slow, daft, can't, can't, can't do what all the others can do.

O is for Oby and Oby is for Obadiah and Obadiah is impossible to spell because no one should be named Obadiah so Oby can spell **O** for Oby and that is all. He copies all the letters of Oby but he can't do it without copying and the letters mean nothing but he copies letters carefully, one after the other, or he gets little Millie to do his work for him as she sits next to him in class and he pays her in sweets and he gives his brother Zach all his pocket money to do his homework for him. His dad is in prison and his mum works all night and she can't read anyway. Right now she is sleeping, sleeping through the day and she won't know to come and get him because their phone has been cut off and her mobile is only to be used for work. Mr Borg is a liar and can't possibly have contacted either of his parents.

The spectre's hand returns to her body. The room is an enormous, white space containing three separate bodies, three entities with no desire to exist within the same universe. The desk is gone. The certificates have vanished. No chair, no carpet, no window, no door.

Only six **O**s float and beckon.

One **O** leads to the Universe called Earth which is a new earth for people who don't belong to this one, where everyone is safe and there is no crying or death or words to fail to read.

One is a place called Air, which is safe because at least you can breathe, but Oby believes no one can survive there without water, unless they are actually a ghost.

Then the **O** of the Universe of Fire, which is the sun, so if you step into that **O** you will immediately be burnt to toast, but you won't feel a thing because it will be so quick.

The **O** of the Universe of Water sounds great if you can swim, but it's highly dangerous because beautiful calm pools become raging white-water torrents that harpoon the atmosphere and giant whirlpools suck and squeeze you into the very centre of their world. It is also freezing because it is too far from the **O** of Fire to absorb any light.

All of these are preferable to the **O** of the Universe of Death and Destruction which is never-ending pain and loneliness.

Finally there is the **O** on the Toblerone sign on Mr Borg's desk. The **O** next to the B of BOrg. That O is the Universe of Uncertainty. Fifty-fifty. It could be good or bad or a mixture of any of the above and Oby could not be sure if he should risk it.

Two **O**s in technOlOgy are close together, with the letter L forming a nose between them, staring hard at him, forcing Oby to look away, because the word is too long and choosing one of the Os against the other would be impossible. Oby eliminates them both, hoping and hoping that they are the gates to Fire and Death.

The **O** in dOne is too obvious because it is the first **O** in the line-up and no one would hide a secret door in the first place everyone comes to. Oby leaves dOne and moves on to bOrg, which is the Universe of Uncertainty and that is surely better than eternal pain but then again, it could *be* eternal pain. On the other hand, at least he knows what bOrg is, because it is definitely Uncertainty.

The **O** in cOllege looks like steps leading up so that could be a good thing and the letter before the **O** in jOseph looks like a slide which is fun, so that could be a good thing, or of course, a slide could be a temptation. A trap.

Oby feels trapped. The spectre is turning, turning towards him. What is she doing? Her glasses catch the sunlight that spears through the window, her pointy-dagger-shoes inch in his direction. Mr Borg sweats with his sticky back against the wall and Oby is alone and has used up all his time. He makes a decision.

He chooses an **O**.

cOllege

Whoosh! The **O** flies towards Oby and wraps its huge lips around him in one huge gulp. Now he is Jonah being devoured by the huge fish, falling through a pulsing oesophagus, down down down!

But the walls are red, so has he chosen fire? No! It can't be because Oby is still alive. Maybe this is a water-shoot soon to burst out into a liquid universe, but no, he can hear something; someone is standing there at the bottom of the shoot with their arms open wide and he thinks maybe the person is his mum when she was younger but it might not be, and behind the person is a field with horses and a skinny dog playing in some hay. There are blue birds everywhere. The sun is shining and Oby is warm and dry and he can feel fresh air and children laughing and he hears a bell ringing. Oby is totally happy and he runs to the dog and hugs him because they know each other and the dog never asks Oby to read what cannot be read or write what cannot be written.

"Drrrrrrr!"

The bell. Oby doesn't react. Above him, Mr Borg is pompous, in charge, pontificating;

"Ok Oby, we'll give you another chance. Tomorrow is a new day. A new start. Ofsted are coming in soon to give us a very special inspection, so you just be good, that's all I ask."

Oby opens the office door and realises the spectre

has gone. He looks up and down the corridor and sees children laughing as they leave for home. He joins the throng of the clever ones, and is bumped by books and bags as they all bottleneck at the exit, then burst out, flowing down the stone steps into the sunshine.

He walks the two miles home alone, but he has saved himself again.

Oby chose the right **O**.

Rosa

Between Two Worlds

Every Saturday she perches on her windowsill, clutches her knees to her chest and waits for her parents. Thirteen years and still waiting. She knows every mark on the glass like it is a part of herself; the stain from her fingerprints is greasy and cannot be successfully erased with Windowlene, so on sunny mornings the light hits the pane at just the right angle, revealing her secret thoughts. Rosa squashes her head down closer to her knees, pushes back her unbrushed brown hair and tilts her eyes against the light until she can decipher what she scrawled last month:

I hate myself: mad mad mental mad:
piss off piss off whoever you are.

She jiggles her neck slightly to admire the miniature oily rainbows swirling delicately through each letter until, many miles above Rosa's windowsill, heaven's clouds smother the sun and the words vanish. Oh well, they'll be back, thinks Rosa. Just because you can't see them doesn't mean they don't exist. Like parents.

Mad mad mental mad.

A bus pulls up at the stop over the road and Rosa cranes her neck to analyse whoever appears from it.

Those two stupid boys again, swinging their soggy swimming towels, always laughing, pushing each other against the privet hedges and bouncing off them like they actually enjoy life. Behind them, alights that lady who lives in the flats, transporting her weird, white mouse-dog in a wicker handbag. Last month, Rosa had witnessed the mini-beast walking, yes walking, on the end of its skinny lead; a hairless Chihuahua runt with a pointed face, a cross between a piglet and a hamster, tripping The Nutcracker Suite across the tarmac.

The lady pauses while the bus departs, then faces the oncoming traffic, with an air of authority. She stretches out her arm as if trying to part the Red Sea, and miraculously, the very first car stops and allows her to step safely forwards. Rosa, from her bedroom sill, can see down into that car, onto the laps of two headless people, a man and a woman, his fingers tapping on the wheel, her hands resting on an open map book. On the nearside, traffic continues past, ignoring the elderly woman, who now hovers on the central white line. She again asserts her authority by raising her arm and this time her face lifts up out of its neck as if to say;

"Stop! It is I!" And there is no choice for the green Mitsubishi Colt, but to screech to a halt, closely followed by a muddy Range Rover Sport, then a multi-coloured van with its own curtains.

The lady ventures forth, eyes forward, ignoring abuse from the Mitsubishi driver, while the white mouse-dog peeps out of its bag, with unblinking black eyes. In seconds the drama is over and Rosa relaxes. No one died.

The landline phone rings downstairs, but Rosa ignores it – it is never for her. Instead she stands with her back bent forward upon her windowsill, opens the top pane upwards and leans out as far as possible. A car passes just below her and a small boy on a booster seat eyeballs her for a split second.

"What're you doing?" questions the child with his eyebrows. Rosa hardens her eyebrows and glares; "What do you care?" And he is gone.

A fat-bodied spider resides in the corner of Rosa's room, where the wall meets the window. Today it has enlarged its web and attached one end to the window. Rosa smirks and pushes the glass out further and waggles it back and forth, stretching the silk rope. The spider clings patiently, until Rosa loses interest and flops backwards off the sill, well-practiced at landing in a heap on her bed, knocking her DS to the floor on top of yesterday's clothes, makeup, DVDs and muddle of homework.

"Rosa?" That irritating voice of too much kindness is at the door asking what she'd like for lunch and if she'd like a friend round later.

"Piss off and push off." Rosa says in her 'most bored' tone of voice, trying to sound hard, hoping that her foster mum, Marianne would go away - which she does. After two years with Rosa, Marianne's learnt one thing; you don't argue or allow yourself to be drawn into an argument and Marianne will do almost anything to keep the peace. In their unspoken rule of separation, Marianne disappears into the garage to sort the recycling and empty the tumble-drier, allowing Rosa to saunter downstairs, rummage through the cupboards for chocolate and biscuits, stuffing crisps into her mouth and using the frother on the coffee machine to transform the last of the milk into milkshake. She adds four spoons of sugar. She leaves the fridge door open, the crisp packet on the floor and chocolate powder sprinkled beneath the microwave.

Normally Rosa stomps back upstairs to make a point, whatever that point might be for today. Normally Marianne hears the stomping, the unspoken signal that it is safe for her to return to the kitchen, to clear the debris. Normally.

But today is not normal because it is another Saturday, when no handsome dad and no wonderful mum appear on the doorstep to rescue her and drive her off into the sunset in their shiny BMW. Rosa abandons the half-consumed milkshake, stomps to the front door, marches out and crosses the road without looking.

"She's a Beautiful Girl," sounds from a radio through the open window of the Specialist Care Home for the Elderly and Rosa takes it personally, lightening her step and tossing her tangled hair several times as her confidence increases.

"I feel like walking the world!" echoes in her mind and Rosa skips a little and almost bumps into a smartly dressed man carrying a black brolly, even though no

way is it going to rain. He politely sidesteps Rosa, but she anticipates this and wrong-steps him, charming him with her fluttering eyelids and disarming smile.

"Er, s'cuse me... you got a quid for the bus? I dropped mine down the drain just now." Rosa points backwards at an imaginary drain in the gutter and the man is embarrassed to refuse a child, thinking what might happen to her if he didn't help her and at the same time his body language says *get me out of here*. He is nervous, not wanting to be accused of assault. He rummages in his pockets and Rosa hears keys jangling against a few coins and holds out her hand like she's Oliver Twist. The man gives her a pound. A second glance at her upturned face and he adds fifty pence then a two pence.

"Great," she says and skips round him without looking back. She repeats this act on two more strangers before boarding the number 41 bus to Morecambe, via Garstang and Lancaster. After paying for her ticket, Rosa has three pounds sixty two pence in her jeans pocket.

She sits halfway down the aisle, as far away as possible from the other passengers, one of whom slings his lazy feet across the entire back seat. Rosa squints at the remains of a squashed fly on the window and lines it up with the passing houses, trees and lampposts. The fly is a laser-cutter; her eye is the control and as she stares, the laser slices through all the buildings and trees and lamp-posts. Behind the bus there is total destruction as the infrastructure along the A6 out of Preston collapses like a domino rally. Rosa knows this without looking back, so she concentrates on holding her head still, with her eye fixed to the fly and beyond.

Lancaster is totally new to Rosa. A whole new world. She abandons the bus at the bus station and sees signposts pointing to Sainsbury's, To the River, Greyhound Bridge, Lancaster Castle, Town Centre and Toilet. Last summer, Rosa had refused to go into public toilets when she was with her foster family on holiday in France, where they'd tried to force her to lock herself into a unisex cubicle containing a hole in the white ceramic floor. Rosa threatened to scream and then she'd cried and spat and jiggled and stamped until Marianne and John caved in and agreed to find "the sort of loo we have at home." They searched for almost an hour, begging at hotels to have mercy, take pity on a frazzled English family. One concierge looked sternly at Marianne, her eyebrows questioning *can't you discipline your own children?* as Rosa marched triumphantly between them, through the gleaming door marked *Femmes*.

There must be a toilet in a castle, deduces Rosa, heading up the cobbled hill. She wishes she'd worn trainers and not her pink flip-flops with the slight heels. She is bursting to go and with no sign of the castle she settles on Pizza Hut at the corner. It's half past four when Rosa brazenly marches through the front door, past the tables and straight to the back of the shop, through a door labelled *Toilets*. Two minutes later Rosa emerges, without washing her hands, and plonks herself at a table by the window, assessing the students and families as they crowd in for food. A young couple makes eye contact and approach Rosa, smiling,

"Do you mind if we sit here?" Rosa silently glares with her coldest eyes, until they obey her command and shuffle off, wondering where to settle. Three teenage girls suddenly flop down at Rosa's table, giggling and waiting for pizza to share. They ignore Rosa, so she's forced to stay put, trapped against the window, pretending not to be bothered. Outside, a scruffy man of unguessable age walks right up to the window staring in, as if Rosa is an exhibit in a zoo. Their eyes meet. He grins, revealing decaying teeth and a dark, craggy tongue. Secure in her enclosure, Rosa continues the cold stare.

"I don't care and you can't touch me," says her face although it resembles a waxwork and doesn't move a muscle.

Then the pizza arrives, extra-large, ready sliced into eight huge wedges with extra everything but no pepperoni, and three diet cokes with straws. Rosa turns to look and when she turns back, the man is twenty paces away, ogling a woman in Accessorize.

The gaggle of girls text and talk and apply lip gloss as they pick at pizza. Rosa watches, and listens and judges. *Geeks* she thinks. *Tarts. Skanks.* Still laughing, the three suddenly depart, leaving two triangles of pizza, stretched pale and cold across the plate. Using her fingers, Rosa scrapes the mushrooms off the cheese and shovels a slice into her mouth; she folds the second piece into a paper napkin and tucks it into her green hoodie pocket. She sucks on a used straw for some melted ice at the bottom of the coke glass before sidling out onto the street. She wanders through narrow alleyways, window shopping, dreaming of nothing, making no decisions. After some time, her legs feel tired and she slips off her shoes to carry them.

The early November sky is darkening. Rosa considers returning to Preston but assumes the police will give her a lift back eventually, as they did last time she absconded, when they found her only three miles from home, down at the docks. They should be searching by now. It's the law. Marianne has to report her missing after two hours.

A group of young men pass Rosa, all chatting at once. Older folk in sensible shoes, anoraks and scarves walk by with a purpose. Children in groups, families, singles, students, indeed every kind of humanity flows in the same direction up the steep hill. Curious, Rosa decides to follow and like a single raindrop she splashes into the stream, flowing with the multitude as they move left and round and up and right and up until before them looms the dark imposing castle. A huge wall with a twin-towered gate-house is set against a clear purple sky. Rosa ignores her bare feet, cold upon the cobbles, as she continues with the crowd swarming around the south side, slowing to shuffle passed the traders selling glow-light strips or pistachio nuts and the local radio personalities doling out free sweets. Shoulder to shoulder the multi-headed millipede inches forward, until a low wall blocks them, so they fan out, tier upon tier, all down the hillside, overlooking the lights of Morecambe Bay that twinkle in the distance. Rosa stands among them, looking and listening and wondering *why*? She imagines something terrible must be about to happen, maybe a flood or a great fire or an alien spaceship, until she becomes afraid of her own thoughts and she turns back against the tide, tears of panic rising in her throat as she pushes her body between elbows, and ducking beneath the linked hands of families, until she is suddenly stuck, pressed against a two metre wall which juts out at right angles from the main castle wall. People surrounding her have stopped.

They are waiting.

Rosa wipes her eyes and glances round, assessing each character. Who will help? Who looks a soft touch? Expertly, she selects a young man with a three-year-old boy on his shoulders.

"Er...s'cuse me?" Rosa stares up, brown eyes begging, at the same time tapping him on his arm, "Can you give me a leg-up onto this wall?" The man nods and smiles. He passes the toddler to his wife, bends down, clasps his hands together to create a step. He lifts her foot and she scrambles up, heaving herself forward onto the ledge. The pizza in her pocket is flattened under her hipbone against the stone. The man hands Rosa her shoes and Rosa wriggles backwards on her bottom until she leans against the mighty castle. Finally, she pulls her knees up to her chin and enjoys the solid wall beneath her feet.

Twenty metres away, above the heads of the crowd towers a high metal post, containing a huge basket of fire; its medieval flame casts halos around the heads of ordinary people. Like a field of dewy spiders' webs they shimmer together; a holy glow of humanity.

Music begins; mysterious classical sounds crackling

from huge speakers. The crowd hushes. Crack! A bright light appears in the sky. Six rockets burst precisely on the beat of the music. Higher and higher fly fireworks that twist, explode, multiply, zoom then splinter and fall. Oooh, aahhh! The crowd cranes its neck, and Rosa is one with them now, as she cradles herself, rocking gently back and forth her chin rubbing against her knee caps. Comfortable above the world, Rosa hugs her shins and becomes a winged princess, flying freely with the rockets and shooting stars. After half an hour, the music crescendos and the sky explodes into five magnificent planet-sized dandelion clocks expanding until they fill the universe. As each seed dies its stardust falls gently towards the earth, while the crowd claps and cheers, then heads for home.

"Hello...hello?" someone is speaking to Rosa and no one should dare do that. Rosa looks down and most people have left, but someone is standing alone in the darkest place, in the crook of the wall. It's a female and the accent is Scottish, or Irish, she didn't know the difference but it wasn't local.

"What?" retorts Rosa, defensive, aggressive, tense.

"You alone?"

"Yeah."

"Want a smoke?"

"Yeah." Rosa shrugs and thinks, *Why not?*

"Get down then."

"No."

The girl, aged about twenty, steps forward, looks up. "What's yer name?"

"Rosa."

"Ha! Weird. Rosa. Rosa what?"

"Rosa Princess."

"Oh freakin' weird! Now get down like I said."

Rosa dangles her legs over the edge and pushes off the wall with her hands, scraping the backs of her thighs and tumbling onto the stranger.

"You stupid cow! You nearly crashed me into the buggy." The girl shoves Rosa against the wall with the back of her arm and holds her face very close to Rosa's, eye to eye and furious. Rosa stands very still and says nothing. The girl laughs and says,

"See my baby? See? See?" She holds Rosa's arm and pushes her head down with the other hand. Rosa stares and blinks through the dark at the old buggy, with its canopy up and a bundle of blankets inside.

"D'ya see it? DO ya?"

"Yes. Yes," replies Rosa, thinking *get me out of here.* The girl suddenly relaxes and smiles;

"Hi, I'm Nula and that's Gaelic for champion! You're all right you are. Come on, you, let's get out of here." Rosa could've run, but not in a strange city, wearing flip-flops in the dark. The girl gives her something... half a cigarette, a thin roll-up with a squashed, blackened end.

"Wait..." she commands, as she lights it with shaking fingers. Rosa has never tasted anything so disgusting, but she drags on it and inhales without coughing. She watches in admiration as her new mate rolls one for herself, at the same time staring at the girl's brown hair.

"Just like mine," thinks Rosa, "but darker and thinner and her skin stinks of stale smoke and urine and old wool jumpers."

Rosa recognises that smell from long ago. It is reminiscent of her pink toddler blanket crumpled on a stained mattress, probably still moulding on the floor of number 5, Stanford Street. Rosa moves nearer to the girl, sniffing inwards, her nose as close as she dares to the sleeve of the grey tee-shirt; and she breathes in the memory of her mother and jumps back! *No! No!* She is screaming at her mother from the back of her brain and the scream came from her tummy but it never left her mouth. Her face looks shocked.

"First time smoke?" mocks the girl and Rosa says nothing. The baby in the buggy never moves. Never makes a sound. The girl shoves the buggy at Rosa and commands her:

"Push!" she says, not expecting to be disobeyed. Rosa clings to the handles and pushes and wonders what to do next.

Rosa has no choice but to follow the older girl without complaint. They walk for ten minutes downhill and away from the main town and although it's not late, it is dark and Rosa feels weary. For an hour they sit on a bench, and Rosa wishes she was in a warm bed, but she never thinks about Marianne or her room in Preston. Nula makes a decision. She jumps up and Rosa is forced to follow, pushing the baby in the buggy. A few cars whizz by heading towards Morecambe, and Rosa wants to raise her arm and stop one, like the lady with the mouse-dog, but she dare not.

"We sleep here." Nula points to a Perspex bus shelter, beside the wide road. Immediately behind the shelter are overgrown shrubs and tangled weeds, then a footpath and behind all of this flows the River Lune, fast and wide and dark as chocolate.

It is four in the morning when Rosa wakes, shivering violently and needing the loo. A street lamp shines on Nula, and Rosa is amazed to see her curled on the bench in the corner, cocooned in two blankets. For the first time, Rosa wants to see the baby, wondering is it a boy or a girl? Did it get fed? Did it ever cry?

"The baby must be wrapped in there with her, 'cos it's definitely not in the buggy. Makes sense to stay warm together," Rosa thinks, as she creeps behind the shelter to squat in the bushes. She shakes so much that she can hardly balance and it's too dark to check for insects. She

wishes and wishes that the police would hurry up and find her; wishes she'd left some clue in her bedroom for Marianne to discover.

Rosa imagines Marianne sleeping soundly, relieved that the vile Rosa has vanished for good this time. She hears her birth-mother saying,

"Well done, mummy's little princess! You got away. No one has the right to care for my baby - only me! You don't have to do anything your foster parents tell you to do..."

Rosa imagines the police understand her now. In her mind the police are with her, wearing their smart uniforms, agreeing with her, saying,

"We get it now. You were right to run away and you have proved that you are strong enough to go back and live with your mum and dad. Your dad was innocent after all... we released him you know. Your mum forgave him and they're going to stay together forever." Then off go the cops to phone the social worker to tell them to send Rosa back to live with them. Right now.

Rosa stands in the bushes, then straightaway squats down again, pressing herself into the dark space, as Nula leaps up from her nest. Even in the fuzzy grey night, Rosa sees the blankets fall on the pavement. Nula spins round, crazy, shouting,

"Where's that freakin' weird kid?" Instinctively, Rosa crouches lower in the bushes, like a hunted animal, backing slowly, slowly, breathing fast and shallow, blowing softly, noiselessly through her mouth.

Nula stomps behind the bus shelter and her shadow, cast by the street lamp, reaches across the scrub and crosses Rosa's dark head. Crazy with rage, Nula rushes to the street, tugging at her own hair, clutching her neck as if a priceless jewel has just been stolen, squinting in the darkness until her eyes adjust, and, in the distance she spies a shadowy figure, someone disappearing into an alley.

"There she is!" Triumphantly Nula tosses her rags into the empty buggy and runs, away, away, away from young Rosa who is trembling in the shadows.

Like a fawn, Rosa curls quietly among the dewy twigs and waits for dawn.

Next thing Rosa remembers are the flashing lights and she's in an ambulance and the paramedics are talking and working and warming her somehow. Then

Marianne is close to her hospital bed and a man is saying,

"She's a lucky young lady surviving a cold night like last night," and Marianne is sobbing, exhausted from her long night spent pacing the streets of Preston, checking doorways and alleyways and keeping in touch with the police. Even Marianne's husband, John, had searched the docks, desperately calling Rosa's name, hollering like a drunkard, because last time the police had found her there, near the cinema, talking to two men, agreeing to go with them for a better life in Manchester.

Julia Sloman from social services arrives. One more night in hospital and she'll be fine, explains the doctor.

"Go home, Marianne, go home," the doctor says. *"Get some rest while you can. You did a good job."* Rosa pretends to sleep, keeping her eyes closed and listening to the love, the concern from the exhausted adults embracing one another and Rosa feels the cool sheets and the warm blankets and hugs her one-eared polar-bear that has mysteriously appeared.

Rosa thinks, *"Take me home Marianne; take me home now and don't ever leave me again."* She longs so much to hug her foster mum and go with her, and feel loved like a real daughter and love her back like a real mother, but Rosa will never hug Marianne. It is too risky. So Rosa stays beneath the white sheets and listens. She knows that Marianne will fetch her tomorrow.

Marianne is always on her side.

Pia

The Broken Compass

Behind the curtains, Pia is alone. In her daydreams she attends the local high school with the lad next door and the girls on her street. In her dreams the lads approve of her tough spirit and girls envy her great figure. In her dreams Pia is popular and fun-loving.

The staff at Taphill School for children with behavioural, emotional and social disorders agree that Pia is ready to move on. She is one of their success stories. Throughout year nine, Pia has transformed her personality from wild cat to quiet mouse, as daily she huddled against the back wall of the classroom scribbling on the worksheets, while watching her classmates disrupt the hours.

Pia begged her support tutor, Miss Rees, to facilitate a move to a mainstream school, namely Christ the King Technology and Maths College, so they visited it together last June, after the final GCSE had been completed and the year elevens had left. Pia tagged behind Miss Rees, wishing she were invisible, envying the confident gangs swarming along the corridors in their dark blazers, white shirts, green and white striped ties and non-fashionable-or-else-you-are-out bottle green trousers.

One visit. Next time will be in September, the first day of year ten and Pia's fantasy of being like everyone else will be realised.

No makeup allowed. No flashy jewellery. No friends yet, but Pia really, really wants to go there. She hasn't bitten anyone for over two years, since her twelfth birthday; and this is what she remembers: Her history teacher, Miss Newton confronts her about her scruffy homework and demands that she rewrites the lot:

"…Read the question for Pete's sake; take that idiotic hat off and while you are at it, you can remove that birthday badge because the pin is dangerous. Oh, and wipe that silly grin off your face!" Pia presses her back against the classroom wall while Miss Newton rants and Pia's mind flashes back ten years. It is her second birthday and her first memory. Pia's mum is screaming in her face, nose-to-nose, because Pia spilt her juice from her grown-up mug with no lid, and in this house there is no mercy for making a mess.

So Pia's twelfth birthday is a school day, and Pia wants to pretend it is a happy day but straightaway Miss Newton ruins it, nagging on and on about completing that impossible homework, so Pia rushes at her like a wild cat and bites her hairy arm.

Behind the curtains, Pia stares at herself in the mirror. It is five a.m. and the sun has not yet risen. She scrapes off the remains of yesterday's makeup, cleansing her panda eyes and dabbing away the blotchy, brown powder to reveal her thin, pale cheeks. She spends almost three hours applying fake tan, dying her strawberry-blonde roots a dull black and plastering a fresh layer of beige foundation across her emotionless face. Pia is happy that Miss Rees is arriving at eight-thirty to give her a lift, to help her cope with Day One.

This week Pia will spend two days in Christ the King, then three back at Taphill School which she now hates. Next week, she will spend three days at Christ the King, then after that it will be four then at last she will be a full-timer, walking to school with her new gang, the cool set, instead of that embarrassing education authority taxi at her front door every morning, beeping its horn impatiently, letting the nosey neighbours know that *Pia attends special school and Pia is never ready on time!* Pia can't wait to study for GCSEs, hang out with the smokers at the gates at break-time, then walk home again, having a laugh. Being normal.

Pia hates smoking, but that's what you do.

Eight thirty-one and Miss Rees is late. Pia's stomach is as tight as menstrual tension so she cannot eat breakfast, but she drinks milk from the carton, while she checks and rechecks her image in the hall mirror. Her new blazer is too broad and feels heavy on her shoulders, but the white shirt looks good and she wonders if anyone will fancy her or find her repulsive.

Eight thirty-three and Pia's mum's mobile suddenly buzzes and rattles like a dying fly on the hall floor. Pia kicks at the piles of mismatched shoes and empty beer cans until she locates it. She reads a text from Miss Rees, which is a long text with proper punctuation, explaining she is stuck in traffic, sorry, don't stress, see Pia soon as possible. Wait there Pia.

Pia tosses the phone across the hall and opens the front door because she really can't wait for Miss Rees and anyway, no other year ten pupil has a tutor tagging along. She picks up her saggy black bag, containing an empty file, a biro, a brand new Nokia, a knife, a can of cola, mascara, eye-liner, compact with mirror, hairbrush and nail file. Pia hesitates and then decides to leave her knife at home, in case Miss Rees checks; and Pia shouldn't need it because today she'll have a whole gang of best mates to defend her. The knife is usually wrapped in a sock at the back of her chest of drawers and no one but Pia ever looks there.

The front door catches in the wind, slams and shakes the thin house walls, and Pia smirks to herself, thinking how annoyed her mum will be to be woken by the bang. She kicks open the gate and stands still for a moment, checks the street up and down for stray dogs, ASBO boys, and Kayleigh Clark, who's not allowed back to school ever and anyway she's seven months pregnant and going to keep it - like they will let her. Not. No one trusts Kayleigh Clark, especially Pia, who once spat in her face at the bus stop and is waiting for Kayleigh to pay her back.

Pia is alone on the street, walking close to the walls and hedges. It dawns on her why kids smoke. They feel scared, vulnerable, don't know what to do with their hands, how to hold their head straight, if their shoulders are level, if their feet point the right way. They develop swaggers or saunters, and kick scraps of rubbish to hide their insecurities. A cigarette replaces the comfort blanket, the sucking-dummy and it sends the message,

"I'm cool, what do I care what you think, look at this stick burning in my hand, don't look at my feet." Pia regrets not stealing a No.10 and a lighter from her mum's bag, but today she's making a new start. And she doesn't usually smoke. Not unless she has to.

The school gates are open and kids of every height and attitude slop through the gap, and Pia realises she is one of them, in their uniform and no one takes any notice of her, which is exactly how she likes it. She clings tight with both hands to her shoulder bag, like a mountaineer grasps a rope, like it will save her from falling and Pia doesn't realise her palms are sweating.

Five wide steps lead up to the towering main doors, where everyone bottlenecks into the corridor, shoulder to shoulder, while a scruffy, balding male teacher repeats robotically, "Single file, single file," with no effect.

She should go to reception but it's too late because the corridor is one way only and Pia is a fish in a fast flowing river. A voice hisses right into her ear.

"*Rat-face.*" At least, Pia thinks it was "*rat-face.*" Can't be *fat face*, she puzzles as she shuffles forward, glad of the fake tan through which no one can read her thoughts. Year sevens turn left, year eights go right. Years nine, ten and eleven shuffle up the stone stairs, following the blue arrows.

Alone in the crowd, Pia tries to blend in, unaware that her makeup breaks the rules and anyone can see she is a new girl. She feels her bag being tugged as if she's a fish on a hook. Then something sharp jabs her hard in the small of her back and Pia reacts quickly, instantly full of rage. She swings round, looks up, checks out the danger. She turns, but is pushed by the crowd, backwards and upstairs onto her bottom and someone treads on her hand, laughing. Pia observes a metal ruler sliding up the sleeve of one boy, vanishing under his watch strap, and the boy shouts down,

"Hey, what ya looking at ya little brown rat!" Pia feels the rage. She snarls as her face is battered by knees, bags of books, coats with buttons and Pia grits her teeth and tries to stand. The bully has moved on and a second batch of kids swear at her to get the hell out of their way. Pia curls up, diminishing her already petite form, tucks her head into her knees, smaller, smaller, compacting until she feels as if every atom of her being will split in two and suddenly she leaps upwards like a nuclear explosion! She jumps up and the top of her head smashes against the chin of the scruffy, balding teacher who was following up the stairs behind her and he flies backwards, arching his neck down, down towards the stone floor below. All the children part as the teacher sails through them and he lands smack on his back. Motionless.

Pia doesn't see this because she has already fled up the last stair and along the corridor and into the classroom that says *Mr Grey, Geography* on the door. She rubs the top of her head as he smiles and says,

"Hello, you must be Pia Lockwood, the new girl. Welcome." He doesn't yell at her to "clean that muck off your face," because it is, after all, her first day. He looks immeasurably kind and Pia immediately imagines he is her own dad. He guides her to her desk as he speaks to a tall girl,

"Mandy, hand out the new school diaries, will you please." The class is quiet because Mr Grey is respected, feared and liked.

Pia sits down, wordlessly. Mr Grey says he'd expected Miss Rees to be with Pia, but Pia doesn't explain, she makes no sound and Mr Grey instantly understands that she is shy and he doesn't draw further attention to her. Everyone waits for the register and usual instructions to the class.

Loud banging on the wall next door sounds like Pia's neighbours fighting or doing DIY or most likely, arguing whilst hammering a nail into the wall. Pia recognises the tell-tale signs of a teacher who has lost control in the first five minutes of the new school year.

Shouting. Screaming. Swearing. A door slams. A boy laughs raucously. Then the whole class laugh.

Mr Grey softly continues the register: Sarah Barnes; Sam Briant; Melanie Dangerfield; Chris Hawkins... he tells the class that Pia Lockwood is new, and it's tough to move into year ten, please make her welcome, and he explains that Sarah Barnes will be her buddy. Pia glances at Sarah Barnes who is un-cool, serious, geeky and obviously doesn't belong to any gang. She wears a school skirt that virtually touches her knees for goodness sake. Pia rejects Sarah Barnes but she smiles briefly, without opening her mouth, trying not to look sarcastic because she needs to fit into this uncomfortable box. Sarah, who is instinctively fearful of Pia, only sits with her to please Mr Grey.

"Hi," she says, in such an awkward way that everyone laughs until Mr Grey silences them with a simple look of his firm eyes. He explains the timetable and apologises because the new gym that was promised over the summer has not been completed, so all indoor games will take place in the hall until further notice. Pia watches a note being passed across the room and she thinks Mr Grey is oblivious; every time he looks down, or at the white board, the note moves a metre. Finally it appears on Pia's desk, just as Mr Grey looks up and he raises his eyebrows, one higher than the other, like Robbie Williams. The note has been folded about eight times, into a tiny package terrifying as a letter bomb, and Pia dare not touch it, so she stares at it petrified, as if it's about to blow up in her face. Mr Grey holds out his hand and quietly says, "Sarah..." and Sarah blushes even though it's got nothing to do with her and she stands and passes the note to Mr Grey. The class glare at her, all eyes accusing *traitor, grass, snitch*. Mr Grey doesn't even read it, just puts it in his pocket and sits back with his eyebrows arched, reading the faces in the room. Pia is mesmerised by his ability to say so little and still keep control and she hopes he teaches her every subject, every day for the rest of her life. At last Mr Grey speaks with quiet authority;

"Mark. Ryan. Sam. See me at break. The rest of you, go to your first lesson. Whole school assembly is at the unusual time of eleven-thirty today, to start off the term." Sarah leads Pia to maths set four; and as there are six sets Pia is amazed to be above the bottom. During maths, the class are restless because there are sirens sounding in the senior yard below, and the teens stare at each other wide-eyed and whisper,

"What is it?"

"What do you reckon?"

"Ask to go to the toilet."

"No, you ask."

Mrs Eccles requests that a boy named John hand out compasses, one between two, while she explains that it's going to be a lot of fun orienteering but first you need to know how to use your equipment. The pupils giggle and nudge each other and Mrs Eccles blushes, realising what she just said. Recovering quickly she adds,

"It's like life. Once you know how to find north, you can't get lost, even in thick fog on a freezing mountain. Pia thinks, *I don't need a compass because I'll never climb a mountain even in sunshine; what's the point?* Pia struggles to find her way through her own life and constantly feels very, very lost, as bereft as a three year old alone at the fairground. What use is a compass in a fairground?

Pia eyeballs Mrs Eccles and Mrs Eccles glances over her oblong-rimmed glasses into Pia's face, which doesn't move a muscle. Unnerved by Pia's expressionless stare Mrs Eccles speaks too brightly,

"John, make sure Pia gets a compass," because John has no intention of providing Pia with one until all his mates have picked the best of the box. John is supposed to count them all out and all back in at the end of the lesson, but Mrs Eccles interrupting him has made him forget where he was up to.

A slim lady in a smart checked suit pops her head round the door without even knocking. Pia's eyes shift beneath her powerful eyeliner and waterproof mascara, suspicious now, because smart-looking people mean trouble.

"Excuse me," the lady apologises with a smile, "just a message for Pia Lockwood..." Pia wants to die because everyone looks straight at her. The lady explains,

"Miss Rees phoned to see if you'd arrived. She's on the M6 stuck behind an accident. She says she will be with you as soon as possible." Pia gulps and nods. The lady beckons to Mrs Eccles who creeps up to hear the private message whispered in her ear. Mrs Eccles looks shocked and pale as the lady departs and once again the class collapses in giggles, except for Pia. Mrs Eccles glares at the group until they fall silent, then she tells Pia,

"That was Mrs Townsend, the Head. Have you met her before?" Pia shakes her head, purses her lips and grips a pencil tight in her right hand, wishing she'd brought her knife. Mrs Eccles hasn't finished speaking. She adds,

"After our lesson there will be a special whole school assembly, which will include a serious message." The class groans, thinking the usual: drugs lecture, respect lecture, while-in-uniform-you-are-the-face-of-our-school lecture.

Assembly.

Pia sits on a plastic chair between Sarah and a boy named Mike who has big feet and trousers so short that his odd socks show and she thinks *what a geek*. Mrs Townsend welcomes everyone, especially year seven, who used to be big fish in small primary school ponds, but are now small fish, minnows, sitting cross-legged along the front three rows. Term is less than three hours old, she explains, and already she has some sad news for her school. Pia is not listening. She daydreams about being adopted by Mr Grey and sees him at his desk writing to the social services on school notepaper, explaining that he and his wife have always wanted a little girl just like Pia and *I am applying to keep her for ever...*

A lanky Asian policeman steps up to the platform and the whole school falls so silent that you'd think everyone had gone home. Pia can hardly breathe just because he is the police. She feels his eyes on her as he talks very carefully about something terrible that happened to Mr Lawson, that may or may not have been an accident on the school stairs and he asks for witnesses to come forward: anyone who saw anything at all should stay behind and help and no one should worry because the school pastoral care worker will sit with them. After several minutes everyone files out in silence and no one stays behind to talk, except the policeman whispering with Mrs Townsend. Pia ignores this because she doesn't care about Mr Lawson and it is nothing to do with her and she doesn't realise that Mr Lawson is the scruffy, bald teacher, from morning duty and that he is now in hospital, in intensive care.

Pia rubs the top of her own head which feels bruised and tender and she considers going home.

A bell screams and rattles and everyone except Pia knows it is lunchtime. She stands alone by a display cabinet full of trophies, not bothered that Sarah has vanished. Pia sees things. Two small boys pass a packet of cigarettes to an older one. A small girl sticks two fingers up at the prefect who bans her from walking the wrong way down the corridor. A male teacher in a black suit winks quickly at a passing year eleven girl and Pia snarls inwardly at him. Pia has no food and no money, but she's not thinking about lunch. She thinks, *So this is it then. This is mainstream.*

Immediately, she no longer wishes to be here. Her dreams shift to hairdressing or beauty or childcare and who needs maths and orienteering for that? Hairdressers don't climb mountains in the fog. Suddenly her new mobile phone sounds in her bag and Pia moves out of the school entrance past a sign that says,

No pupils allowed beyond this point during breaks

As she walks, Pia holds the phone to her ear.

"Where the hell are you, you stupid little menace? Stop wandering the streets and making a flaming nuisance of yourself – there's stuff to do here. Get your..." Pia's mum yatters on and on, fuelled by alcohol and stress and Pia moves the voice from her ear to her trouser pocket, so she can't see it, knowing it will only stop when it runs out of credit. Pia sees a police car parked in the disabled parking space by the entrance to Mrs Townsend's office.

The Asian policeman is sitting in it making notes in a little book and speaking into his radio. He looks up suddenly and his eyes lock with Pia's. Alone in the car park, Pia is uncertain, because she's not sure if she's doing anything wrong, and her mind rewinds and whizzes through the morning; Miss Rees being late, the squash of kids on the stairs, the mocking voice - "Rat-face," the bump on her head; the disappointment of being paired with Sarah, the kind and gorgeous Mr Grey, Mike's odd socks in assembly. Nothing seems to be her fault and yet...

Pia still has the feeling that she is the cause of some kind of trouble and she wants to apologise to someone for something, to somehow clear herself of any blame for anything, to be reassured that she is not in trouble, that she has offered no one a reason to scream at her or hit her or banish her. The policeman clambers out of his car, leaving the door open as he walks towards Pia.

He knows, he knows, he knows... but what does he know? Pia's head is pounding. He stops ten paces off and questions the little girl.

"Are you all right, young lady?" His face is gentle so Pia wants to tell him, *no, I'm not all right. I don't know what to do, I might've done something wrong but I can't work it out.*

Her mother is still yapping and suddenly Pia is aware of something else in her pocket and in a panic to think of a reply, to offer a reason for her flustered reactions, she pulls the thing out, and it is a compass. She inspects the face of the compass and the pointer shakes erratically between North and West. She holds out the compass to the policeman and stammers,

"I...I...I think I took this away by mistake." The policeman shows suitable concern and steps forward; he reaches out to the child and takes the little blue scratched object into his own hands. He scrutinises it, while Pia's heart beats double-time terrified. After ten long seconds he offers it back, smiling warmly, but Pia doesn't trust him.

He says, "I wouldn't worry yourself about this... don't think they'll be missing it too much. It's broken. The magnetism is up the creek. Useless. Look!"

He holds it under her nose and the thing is just a broken thing.

"Oh," says Pia, as if she understands. She wants to ask,

"What were you on about in assembly?" but she doesn't dare. The thoughts in her head don't connect properly in her mouth. Her own voice sounds terrible to Pia, like it fills too much air and gets in everyone's way.

"What's that noise?" he asks friendly, feigning surprise.

"Um...iPod," lies Pia, gripping the mobile in her hand and wishing her mum would dry up and hang up.

"We didn't have those things when I was at school," he says cheerily. Pia raises her eyebrows and gives him her teenage *what an idiot* look, so the policeman says he'd better be off and adds,

"You have a good afternoon young lady!" and before you know it, he is in his car heading off to the station. Pia ignores her rumbling tummy and walks, skinny as a stick, down the school drive and no one runs after her to bring her back. She is passing the Co-Op when she recognises Miss Rees' blue Fiesta speeding by, towards the school gates. She sees Miss Rees gripping the steering wheel with both hands held tight together on top, as if to make the car go faster, and her knuckles are white as mushrooms. Her hair is piled high today, like pale gold candyfloss and Pia thinks she looks weird and posh and she realises how idiotic she'd have looked, traipsing behind Miss Rees on her first day at mainstream school.

Pia stares at the Co-Op window displaying its mega-sized chocolate bars and she feels queasy. The phone in her pocket falls silent, but Pia doesn't notice.

Minutes later, Pia pushes at her front door and it's not locked, and her mum is asleep on the hall floor, mouth agape, mobile in hand, surrounded by empty cans of White Label. Pia steps over her and switches on the light in the front room because no one ever bothers to open the curtains; then she flings her new blazer onto the kitchen floor and rummages in the cupboard for Pot Noodles. Immediately the lights flick off because the metre is empty and there's nothing to feed the metre so Pot Noodles is off the menu. Pia eats four Jaffa Cakes and a packet of Co-Op crisps. She sits on the kitchen floor and skims through a worn copy of OK magazine that her mate 'borrowed' from the hairdresser's. She feels angry with Ashley Cole for having an affair and admires Jordan for caring for her blind kid and wonders what Posh said when Beckham got his tattoo after she begged him not to. Pia would like a tattoo of a butterfly, but she's afraid of the muscleman image etched on the tattooist's shop window in the high street. Also, Pia had read somewhere that if you tattoo your neck, when you get old, the tattoo fades and crinkles onto your wrinkles and there is nothing you can do about it.

There's a knock at the front door. Pia creeps across the lounge and incredibly slowly, she peeks through a cigarette-burn hole in the curtains and spies Miss Rees on the doorstep, with another woman from Christ the King. Pia backs up softly, barefoot, sidles into the hall from where she can hear the women talking on the front step. She holds her breath and presses her ear to her cupped hand against the plastic front door:

"Yes, they all said it was her. She attacked him – apparently pushed him downstairs with both hands."

"Let me handle it. I'll talk to her. It will have been her. She tends to react badly..."

Pia gently, gently lifts the security chain on the door and noiselessly slides it in place. More knocking. More urgent knocking. Miss Rees clearly says,

"I sometimes go round the back..." Pia leaps like a gazelle over her mum and stabs the sole of her foot on a piece of broken mug. In the kitchen she hastily checks the lock on the back door, glad that the broken, brown bamboo blinds cover the glass pane. Through the blinds Pia sees the rough outline of Miss Rees, and she smiles to herself because Miss Rees will be wearing beautiful shoes and stepping on soggy old rugs and other unmentionable rubbish stuck to the yard stones. Pia tiptoes back to her sleeping mum and prises the mobile out of her hand, just as it starts to buzz and shake and play God Save Our Gracious Queen. Quickly Pia switches it off. Outside Miss Rees is saying,

"They must be out and the phone is off… it'll be out of credit."

Pia flies upstairs, leaving small splodges of blood in her tracks. She grabs her teddy and her pillow and locks herself into the bathroom. She squeezes into her special place, beneath the lowest rungs of the linen cupboard among the old pillows and towels.

Somewhere in the next street an ice-cream van plays Greensleeves, a lullaby for Pia who falls asleep, dreaming that Mr Grey is buying her a large vanilla softie with a flake and fairy sprinkles. She tastes it. It is delicious and in her dream she twists around and sees a boy in a blazer, wearing odd socks and sneering at her.

"Rat-face," he cackles, so Pia stares hard at him, eyeball to eyeball, raises her dripping ice-cream and shoves it right up his nose!

In her safe place, the child smiles in her sleep.

Blake

Diamondman

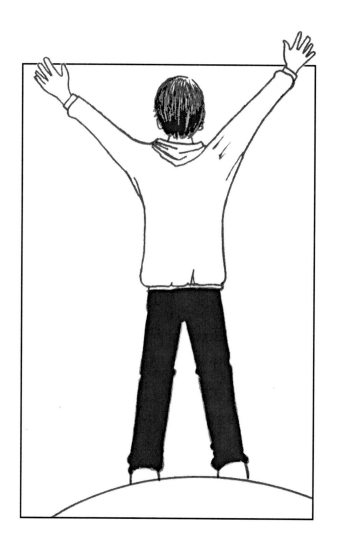

It's amazing stuff.

The laminated poster on the wall explains that the planet Jupiter is composed of helium gas and hydrogen just like the sun! Right in the centre is iron silicate (whatever that is) surrounded by liquid metallic hydrogen. All around the outside are water droplets or ice crystals and winds that blow more strongly than a hundred hurricanes. Jupiter is surrounded by sixteen moons and massive ghostly clouds and one of the clouds alone is bigger than three planet Earths and looks like a giant red spot which can be seen from a telescope. There's so much radiation up there that it would kill a person, *even a thousand people*, outright. In July 1994, there was a comet called Shoemaker-Levy 9 which collided with Jupiter with spectacular magnificent incredible effects that could be seen from Earth. No one has ever dared venture towards it, even with all the ultimate protective gear, radiation defenders and life-preserving powers provided by NASA. No-one.

And now here am I.

I spent nine years and seven days travelling to Jupiter encased in this, the latest model of the Apollos

Maximus; christened by its creator as *The Silver Ghost.* My partner, Peter Tanner of Kentucky USA, was ten years my senior until silently, he died at my side two years ago. Peter remains encapsulated in his spacesuit, looking like a shop dummy with a light tan, staring ahead into the universe. He'd never had a beard 'til after his death when the hairy stubble crept out of his chin for five millimetres, then stopped. Creepy! The day Peter died he looked about thirty-five years old, and three days later he looked fifty-five. Hey, I feel alone, but not lonely; crazy for companionship, but not mad in my mind.

I once told everyone who'd listen that "when I grow up I want to be an astronaut," but no one believed me because I so rarely went to school, preferring to hang around with street gangs in Manchester. I'm just a small guy so the older kids posted me through high windows, encouraging me to lift front door keys from pegs in the kitchen, sapphire rings from bedside lockers, gold watches from bathroom ledges and leather wallets from men's jackets hooked on the back of bedroom doors. I let myself out through the front door, swaggering in my *I'm invincible* way while waiting for my reward.

So what? I can still read and write because I went to Primary School – in fact I was in five different primary schools, but I totally missed year six because mum took me and my sisters to live in a caravan with a traveller called Flint, a bloke she met in Lidl. Flint smelt of Own-Brand lemon washing-up liquid with essence of ground-in-to-skin horse muck and when mum was somewhere else, Flint told me that if I'm out on one of my jaunts and they decide to move on, tough. They will leave me to it and it will be up to me to find them myself. And that's exactly what happened, except I didn't try to find them. Where do you start when you are twelve years old? So that's how I ended up in care. And social moved me up north to keep me safe from gangs. Or so they thought.

Anyway, I'm travelling at incredible speeds, but I feel like I'm floating, drifting among the stars, and Jupiter is there, full in my face but still far away. It is the huge and unexplored planet, eleven times bigger than the earth and four hundred and eighty two million miles from the sun! It's not as dark as you'd imagine, because everything out there reflects the sun, or light from other suns and space is a terrestrial junk yard, full of flying objects, meteors, shards of metal, stars that chuck out dust and pieces of rubbish. The whole outer-atmosphere is bluish-green and smells of beef. Yes really! Don't you try to tell me the odour is Peter's body stinking of dead meat, because the atmosphere smelt of beef before Peter died and anyway, Peter is totally encased in his suit and nothing leaks out; not a thing.

I push a few buttons but there is nothing to control, except the music centre, because our course has been set by Earth Control and I have no choice. Jupiter or bust. The story goes that they found traces of dried-up oceans on the Moon, then bacteria on Mars, then a satellite picked up some ancient messages from Jupiter, that came bouncing over a galaxy or two like a tennis ball in slow-mo, and these messages were finally deciphered by the most finely chiselled brains on Earth. Turns out that they are talking about a huge diamond on Jupiter, created by dust, gases and fire from the sun. This diamond is not a single prism-shaped rock like one you might nick from a jeweller's, but a coil, a string of crystal boxes melting together which cool as Jupiter spins, and this coil forms a spiral three times round the planet and what's more it is still forming right now, this minute.

I see that greedy look in your eyes, so don't all rush at once, like the race for Klondike Gold! That gold was irresistible. Thousands upon thousands rushed from all over the world to seek their fortune in the Yukon Territory and it is a true fact that sixty-eight lucky punters returned as millionaires.

Countless men and women died in that treacherous adventure to a frozen land where mighty walls of rock and earth loomed grey above their heads. The papers reported,

"They are human beings but never did men look so small."

You might just be able to steal yourself a couple of huskies to sledge you and your sieve across some freezing snow in Alaska, but you can't jump in any old rocket to Jupiter and pan for diamonds. Take it from me, fetch your money from the government, why don't you, and when they say *"you sponger, get a job,"* tell them it's better to be a living beggar on earth than a famous astronaut like Peter Kennedy, floating dead as a dummy in outer space.

What's the point of getting out of bed at six-thirty every morning to go to work, when you can open a giro on your own doorstep, and cash it, smoke it or shoot it up in a weekend?

Ssh! I hear voices now. Men and women in debate, but only a few words reach my inner consciousness;

…What about his victims? He thinks he's invincible. Needs more than a warning… My view? He needs a short sharp shock… It's about time he realised…

And I *do* realise that a huge shadow is enveloping me, and ice clings to the windows of the Silver Ghost, with frozen, jagged teeth that threaten to penetrate the safety of my capsule. Out there, I wouldn't last a splintered millisecond, so I'm grateful for this brilliant place, with its permanent temperature set at moderate and my comfortable seat. I focus straight forward to the sparkling planet ahead.

But it's so dark now. Landing soon. Countdown to landing. Brace yourselves. We're landing now.

"Hey," I call to Peter, "this is it mate. One giant step for mankind and all that."

Last February, it was my seventeenth birthday and that was a bad day, man you'd better forget it. Instead, I'll tell you about the time when I was four.

I am all alone in the flat as usual; messing about. It is the days of video. I pick a PG called 'Apollo 13' starring Tom Hanks and I jam it into the machine. I sit cross-legged, mesmerised as I watch men walk on the moon. DVD hadn't even been invented back then, but you could go to another planet. So I see these American guys in puffy white suits land on the moon and someone says, "One giant step for mankind." Or was Apollo 13 the film where they messed up and someone says; "Houston we have a problem?" I admit my memory is fuzzy and the giant step didn't happen in that film… it can't possibly have been Apollo 13 – they failed didn't they? Mission unaccomplished! I must have heard it somewhere else and over the years all the moon landings and space trips and famous words merge in my mind to form one incredible story. The structure of my own DNA is triumph, disaster and failure, and this powerful rope cannot be pulled apart. Failure is not an option.

I was four years old and can't guarantee where I heard it, but I memorised the giant step and repeated it every time I got out of bed. I still do it today. Every time my feet leave the mattress and hit the floor I say, "One giant step for mankind." It makes my day happen. It gives me reason.

Since that day I've tried to compose some memorable words for my own personal, famous moment, when the whole world knows my name, even in Australia and China. Even the whole of Man United will know that I am Blake Connell, conqueror of outer space. Right now, I sense my moment approaching and my heart throbs against my neck. I'm pumping up words for the record, and I can visualise them in bold print in the headlines and even my mum will be proud that I am famous. What will I say when I step off this magnificent machine, the first human, the first child, the first teenager to speak aloud on Jupiter?

"My photoreceptor is changing structure to receive the new light." Too concocted.

"Who on Earth can truly know what I now understand?" Too emotional.

"Diamondman has landed!" I nod. Now that sounds impressive.

I never take that first giant step because Apollos Maximus crashes. It explodes into a trillion pieces, refracting century old sunlight, like aluminium foil twirling down from the ceiling, spinning like sparkling sycamore seeds, the way it does when the new President is announced, or the winner of Mr Universe, or You've Got Talent. Apollos Maximus, the Silver Ghost, totally misses the soft, gassy planet and strikes the corner of the magnificent diamond coil, which cannot be damaged except by another diamond of equal hardness. The Silver Ghost capsule smashes silently, because there is no sound in space. Peter vanishes, still attached upright in his seat, already miles from me, floating, forever staring and unburied. And I have no broken heart or tears, because I too am dead.

I, Blake Connell, am obliterated.

I am aware of voices echoing in the spaces around my head; they sound like men... like women. *What is happening? Can anyone save him? What is your plan?*

I will transform myself.

Diamondman has landed and I am massive. Muscle-sculpted ice forms my biceps and triceps and calves and thighs. Huge ski-boot-shaped feet stand solid, supporting my towering frame. My thorax is shaped like a giant insect, segments of cut glass are wrapped round in movable transparent blocks, one on top of the other, all linked by a sparkling backbone to my square neck, which is magnificently chiselled with vertical cuts, perpendicular veins, leading up to the face of a hero.

Diamondman. Born of Jupiter and Earth.

The components of The Silver Ghost have fused with gas and dust and sunlight from the diamond coil, to form this indestructible mega-man who stands before you alive with the breath and the heart of a boy.

And it is as Diamondman that I, Blake Connell aged 17, of number 10, Canada Street, stand before my judge. He is wearing a wig and a gown, because this is a crown court.

Who do you think you are, with that weird thing on your head? God or what? Last year it was youth court and there you have three magistrates who look like ordinary guys with no wigs, because wigs scare kids like clowns scare kids. Some people think we ought to be scared because of all the bad stuff we do, scared to death, literally, because they can't hang us. Bring back the birch whatever that is.

I stand but I do not speak, because no one asks me to. To my left is a man in a dark suit, who tells the court my name, address and situation. He says I am under section 20, meaning my mum is still in charge of me but doesn't do a good job of it, so I have to live in a care home. How good is that? I live in a care home with good food, clean sheets and trips out to learn motorbike skills or to the ice rink, but I can go home whenever my mum agrees and play on the Play-Station all night without restriction, smoke pot and watch films and who cares what rating? When I'm bored I go out, or at least when I'm not tagged. I go out and I find my mates. Mostly, they're like my real family. They do half the crimes in the city and they teach me all they know because I'm cool and I'm small enough to be pushed through high windows. They pay me in pot, and call me pot-head, but I don't even use it for myself so I flog it to kids as they come out the school gates, and I make a few quid for chocolate and war games. I learnt all this in Manchester, and these skills have so far been useful in my new town.

To my right stands a woman in a suit and incredibly high heels, wearing superman specs and holding a clipboard. She goes on about my terrible upbringing, mum on drugs, dad in prison, two sisters they call vulnerable, me with no chance. The man on my left yats on about how last year I wasted my one-to-one education with the tutor I didn't get out of bed for; the woman from Addaction who's s'posed to guide me away from booze and pot, who I ignore; and Paul from the Youth Offenders Team who's been guiding my family all my life and even before I was born. Paul is getting a bit sick of the Connell family and I think he kind of has a soft spot for me, but this latest episode with the gun has fazed him, and he doesn't know how to help me anymore.

"Paul's at his wits' end," says Mark. Mark is my key worker at the care home, who is pretty good most of the time, when he's on duty. He used to be a mechanic, but one day he decided to help guys like me, as if I need help, so he is re-training as a youth worker. Why does he need training? Just come in to the care home, sit around, make a few phone calls, go home. Cushy job. I could do it, but they wouldn't pay me enough.

I have to confirm that it is me they are on about, so I nod but the judge says, "Speak up, young man," so I say, "Yes," loudly but it comes out all squeaky and I sound like a smack-head and not at all like Diamondman.

I glance round suspiciously, but to my relief no one seems that bothered about my weedy voice. The ice on my muscles is melting from the sun's heat, and dripping onto the shiny floor. My powerful thorax is pumping with adrenalin, tension-alert to react to any sign of danger. My strength is my youth and my power is in Diamondman, within whom no weakness is found. No one tells Diamondman what to do. The voices around me twist out of tune, like a radio on a bad frequency, riding on waves that distort through the floating debris of Apollo Maximus.

A posh woman is saying, "*...limited understanding of the world around him, and he struggles to comprehend the consequences of his action... attention deficit... limited vocabulary... special needs...*" She doesn't even know me.

Ask *me* why don't you? Ask me about space and time, and chemistry and physics and comics and heroes. Ask me stuff you don't know, but I do. And be amazed. Be very amazed. But you will never ask me because you think you have me sussed and you don't really want to know me, not the real me.

I didn't do much school so I must be stupid. I only got a couple of entry level certificates from my tutor, so I must be illiterate. I have an ASBO or three so I'm a criminal. I don't have a job so I'm lazy. And I got a girl pregnant so I'm a drain and the tax-payer has to cough up for the kid and anyway there's no proof it is mine. Lisa doesn't want anything to do with me ever again, and only went with me for a dare and is hanging out with Kieran and didn't tell her mum it was me, 'cos her mum warned her not to go with me and I would only bring trouble. Yes, man. I gave them trouble all right and Lisa is a B.I.T.C.H anyway. Dog.

Whatever.

That Connexions woman asked me last year, what do I want to do at college? I said, "*Space Study.*" She laughed like it was a joke, trying to pal up to me. Who does she think she is mocking my ideas? Don't ask if you don't want to know. She was sarcastic and said, "*Spaced-out-study, more like*" and suggested I do plastering or mechanics, silly bitch. She should know they won't let me do mechanics at college because when I was fourteen, I nicked a car. It was a manked-up five year old black Fiesta and I didn't even keep it. Gave it to Aaron Noblet, who crashed it into the wall of the Fox Restaurant, then legged it. When they arrested him, he blamed me and my prints were all over the place.

Justice was done, because he's dead now. OD-ed or something and I miss him not. No, man. Come to think of it, Aaron went with Lisa and he could be the dad so how can CPS get money from a dead bloke? Thinking of Aaron reminds me of my travelling companion, the deceased Peter Tanner and I wonder if he's arrived at Saturn yet, which is the next planet from Jupiter in the solar system.

I feel rhythm, music in my head and Diamondman moves to the beat, yes man... *stand close to me, don't let me be alone...* but Peter cannot hear my mind, even though I am trying to make a prayer, a noise no man can hear but is God really there... *it's ripping me apart...* the Silver Ghost is smashed to smithereens... *red red wine, help me take a stand...*

I hear the Judge.

"Six months," he declares but I don't believe him. Someone takes my arms and leads me where I do not want to go, and what to do I just don't know and my mum never came to court, it would make her too distraught;

...red red wine... the fault is never mine... now I'm going down, no more hanging round town... *stay close to me, I need to feel fine...*

My feet are so heavy but I move a step. Step down. No one asks me to speak. No one asks,

"What are your last words? The ones for the paper?"

The Sun is waiting.

Give me some time; got to clear my mind...

Then it comes to me. This is my moment to speak or forever be forgotten.

I am standing on Jupiter. I lift my head towards Saturn, with my muscular arms raised in triumph. My voice echoes strong across the courtroom and I announce the arrival of a new superhero.

"Diamondman has landed!"

Being Forgotten

Behind the Stories

You don't need a degree in psychology to know that everyone prefers to be loved rather than to be hated. You prefer that others are kind to you and are not mean or cruel; that a child (even an adult child) has an innate desire to please their parents and longs for their mother to show pride in that artwork or their father to cheer for them on the sports pitch.

When a baby cries at night, most parents meet its needs with tenderness, however grumpy and overtired they feel. A baby is sensitive to atmosphere; it hears the laughter and the arguments, the noise and the silence and learns to differentiate the difference between safety and danger, between security and uncertainty. A counsellor friend once told me,

"I give my children night feeds even though they are now sixteen and seventeen years old or more." She was referring to those tense times, when students Susan or Rob come home late, mum and/or dad are already asleep or more likely half-asleep, worrying and listening for the slam of a taxi door or the click of the latch to assure them that their child is safe.

This counsellor allowed her teen-child to enter her bedroom at midnight or later and chat about their night out, who did what and why and where and the trouble they just narrowly avoided. Of course the child is not starving for food, but those ten minutes of time feed them with the parent's interest, care and kindness. It is not a time for opinion or argument or for that matter, counselling, ("Oh Susan, you shouldn't have done that!") It is a time to simply listen and maybe say, "Good night, sleep well!"

What's the big deal? The big deal is that this isn't rocket science; it is about strengthening relationships and keeping open the bridge between the generations. It is a simple pattern of listening and caring and finding positive things to say. It is about being consistent in meeting the child's emotional needs.

Is this just idealistic? Surely teenagers are inherently difficult and nothing a parent or teacher can do makes a blind bit of difference? If we cannot attain our ideals, our perfect child, the one that never strays, never rebels, never fails, achieves all the targets, then do we simply give up trying to support and guide? Do we act like Christopher Robin and Winnie the Pooh who chucked their stick into the river hoping it would float and not get stuck somewhere under the bridge?

So we wait anxiously on the other side of the bridge to see if the stick emerges in one piece. And if it doesn't?

Well, that's life. The stick got stuck. The point is that our children/pupils are not sticks to be chucked into life's river, sink or swim, while we anxiously stand by and watch. Anxiety and worry never changed anything for the better. We need to help our youngsters balance the odds in their favour.

Inevitably, countless youngsters are treated like sticks at some stage of their lives. Many adults, (including professionals) assume that if a teenager is "going to do *that* anyway," (sex, drugs, drunkenness, swear, miss school), then there is no point in intervening by suggesting an alternative activity or offering guidance that the teenager will blatantly ignore.

"Being Forgotten" highlights some aspects of behaviour that may emerge if a young person's emotional needs are not met. A healthy society is all about the teamwork of parents and teachers and every adult involved in a child's life. You have a part to play and so do I. This is not about the power of positive thinking, but the success gained by our positive actions and positive speaking. It is often said that for every negative comment a person receives, they need at least seven positive ones to counteract the damage caused.

So what to do? The young person who throws a chair in class needs discipline. True. But what kind of discipline? Exclusion? Shouting? Name-calling? Lines? Who really has the time to give the night feed and to listen to the child? It requires hours, weeks maybe years of consistent time to work towards healing the damage, not of the broken chair, but the battered life; time that most of us claim we do not have, but if we choose to make an effort, we can all play our part:-

Firstly, by not contributing to the damage in the first place; so it follows that our own restrained behaviour and use of words is vital. How often have you heard an adult say, "That @*!^*! child won't stop swearing!"

Secondly, if a teenager is moody, angry, rude or even criminal, then a kind word (even just "Hi!") or a smile won't do any harm and only takes a second. A positive comment ("Didn't I see you in the cricket team last week? Well done!") does not mean that you condone their bad behaviour – on the contrary it may make it more likely that the recipient will receive your discipline with better grace.

Let's try to relieve the pressure of targets to be attained or missed, and re-introduce the joy, (yes, joy) of reading, painting, music, drama, history, science, the natural world and the list is endless.

What goes on in the mind of a child/teen? They can make powerful decisions deep within themselves and not tell a soul. The following three examples are all true, and occurred in different primary schools over twenty years ago. The children concerned were negatively affected for the whole of their school life.

Scene One: Tracey's Story

"My two daughters were born eighteen months apart. When Rosie was in reception she brought reading books home and we read them together with her pre-school sister Charlotte. Charlotte 'accidentally' learnt to read. More importantly she developed a love of learning and was excited when she too could start primary school. In her first week Charlotte asked her new teacher for a book to take home. The teacher said,

"Oh no, you can't have a book because I haven't taught you to read yet!" The teacher may have had good reasons, but Charlotte immediately felt disappointed by school and her love of learning went out like a light. She was a bright child and didn't have to work hard to succeed. She is in her twenties now and has never regained that initial joy of learning."

Scene Two: Dave's Story

I was seven years old when our family moved from Birmingham to Manchester. In Birmingham, I had excelled at school and enjoyed both reading and story-telling, so I was happy to discover that my new school followed the identical reading scheme, albeit several books behind. My new teacher gave me four books from this series to read at home. I turned up to class the next day and told my teacher I had read them all. She told me,

"That is impossible! Take them home again and read them properly." Bewildered, I did as I was told. Again I returned to school and told the teacher I had read them. She refused to believe me.

"You can't have done. Do it again." I couldn't understand why she didn't believe me because I wasn't the sort of child who would lie, so at seven years old I decided that reading was not worth the effort and did not read another book throughout my whole school life. I sat my GCSEs a year early – even English literature. Yes, I wrote essays on Macbeth and To Kill a Mockingbird but I never read the actual books.

When I left school after A-levels, the spell was broken and I suddenly decided to read a science fiction book called The Chrysalids by John Wyndham. The floodgates were opened and I read over one hundred books in a year!

Scene Three: Bhupinder

I was in year six and I hated maths because I never got a gold star. The older I got, the harder maths became and the more unlikely I was to succeed. One day a trainee teacher arrived. She asked me why I didn't try in maths so I told her I was rubbish at it. The next day we handed in our homework. This new teacher marked it and I was amazed because I got every sum right. There it was. A gold star. I loved maths after that and always put in my best effort. I realise now that the teacher assigned me a much easier task than the rest of the class. As an adult, maths still doesn't come naturally to me, but at least I am not scared of it, like some people.

What will you say when your child or your pupil surprises you with a moment of excellence or a rush of enthusiasm?

"That's not what I have planned to do. Go away, I'm the teacher!" or…

"Well done. Let's chat about that right now!"

I wonder?

The Story Behind the Stories

None of the stories is based on a single character or event, but each was inspired by events and conversations with some of my pupils and foster children. All the stories are fictional but like all good fiction, there is more than a grain of truth at the core.

 ## *Esau*
Being Forgotten

The Character

The name Esau originated in Hebrew and its primary meaning is 'to do,' so I chose this name because Esau means doer, a person who does something. In this story, Esau represents a certain type of child, who presents as quiet, maybe studious, not part of the cool crowd. As they say in the fashion industry,

"One minute you are in, the next you are out!" But Esau has never been 'in.' He doesn't desire to be 'in.' He simply takes one day at a time and gets through it.

The majority of teens believe the world revolves around them and Esau is no exception. He stands at the bus stop and on the face of it he appears dull and disinterested compared to his lively, excitable peers. Their habit is to ignore Esau and Esau accepts this.

I like the idea that Esau is in his own imaginative world of fame and power. You could be teaching Esau Pythagoras' theorem, but Esau would be scoring the winning goal for England. The foundation of the story is that, on this one day, Esau's choice of action catapults him into realising that there are people 'out there' who are more forgotten or ignored than himself and the world no longer revolves around him. He sees the 'monster' as a real person and in so doing, shows us how he, Esau, deserves to be treated; as a human being with feelings.

Esau's Theme
Loneliness

This is a complicated, multifaceted emotion with varied causes. It is a subjective experience. If a person feels lonely then they are lonely for their own reasons. Someone who is alone is not necessarily lonely, yet a person can stand in a crowd and feel acutely lonely. Most of the teens represented in this book could be said to be suffering from loneliness to one degree or another.

Esau possibly suffers from social loneliness although strictly speaking, Esau does not experience alone-ness because he lives with his family; he is also a member of a school and converses with people on a daily basis. However he is not one of the in-crowd. Within his school, Esau will not be the only one who is an 'outsider', but to introduce two 'outsiders' to each other is unlikely to solve the problem and unlikely to result in real friendship.

A child who resolves to befriend Esau, should this be possible, may not necessarily relieve the lonely condition. Esau's introverted character tends towards loneliness and he tests out this isolation by standing still while those around him move. It is fascinates Esau that this decision goes unnoticed. He abandons routine with no consideration for the possible consequences; that he might court danger or that someone might report him missing and panic his family.

In everyday life, Esau doesn't think about his mum or his sister like this. It never occurs to him that his mum might shop or clean and his sister has a life at college or with her mates. Esau does thinks about Cyclops. He even defends her fiercely. He defends her by keeping her existence a secret, even though he would have been better to talk to a teacher or his parents so that they could get Cyclops the support she needed.

Negatives

- Esau is seemingly unaware of danger.

- He never talks about his experience with Cyclops. Perhaps Esau fears being misunderstood or mocked and he has learnt that there is no point in sharing his day with anyone.

- Local youth do know about Cyclops but have labelled her a witch and she has probably been the subject of their mockery and distain.

Positives

- Esau observes the behaviour of others. On this particular day he realises that others exist outside of his world, starting with the passengers in the plane. Esau becomes emotionally aware of the needs of someone whose situation is diametrically opposed to his own. That is; the person is female, an adult in distress whose history is unknown.

- Esau is not an active type of person. However on this one day he does something admirable and in so doing Esau reveals his innate kindness. He wants to help Cyclops in spite of the obvious revulsion he feels to the sight and the smell of her. He doesn't save her life or report her plight but he does what he is able to – he gives her his packed lunch and his sweatshirt.

- Esau does more than this. He enters into conversation, albeit awkward and jokey! At least he tries to be friendly. His actions are totally altruistic.

- Esau copes with his predicament by employing his imagination. He fantasises about the identity of the 'Being', a strategy which helps Esau to face his natural fear of the stranger.

- Esau has imbibed some knowledge from school (eg war poets) but with limited comprehension. He uses the information to feed his imagination rather than securing the knowledge for its own sake. Fact and fantasy are still confused and Esau enjoys this.

- To his classmates he is a fool – someone to be laughed at or avoided but Esau is the best kind of hero; the one who doesn't realise his own kindness; the one who does what he does just because it needs to be done.

Discussion

- How do you think you would react in a similar situation?

- Is it easier to give someone money or conversation?

- When a teacher realises that someone doesn't fit into their peer group what concerns should they have, if any?

- If we knew Esau, maybe as a member of our group or class, how might we support him or do you consider that he would be best left alone in his own world?

- Esau embodies the statement: "You can't judge a book by its cover." Is that true? Or do you think you can spot the daydreamer in the pack?

Kirja
The Scent of A Mother

The Character

Kirja is a girl, aged fourteen, who appears happy and without self-pity. Her mother has abandoned the family home after her dad lost his legs in an accident at work. Even though there is professional support for dad, Kirja is still his primary carer. She spends most of her time in her own room, her safe space, where the constant in her life is Johnny Depp. The chaos within Kirja stems from the realisation that her mother has chosen to abandon her for what she considers a more important life, possibly in politics.

One of our foster children occasionally wrecked his room and spent ages re-ordering it. We were already asleep one night when we heard the sound of crashing and objects being thrown. Later, the child re-ordered all his possessions into neat lines alone the windowsill and in the locker. We learnt that this is not unique behaviour but a way of coping with internal chaos and confusion. Punishment, reprimand, anger – none of these options offer sensible solutions to this behaviour. This was a time for silence, for acceptance, to be patient and simply to move on.

Another of our foster children was, like Kirja, obsessed by a particular film star, which, up to a point is normal behaviour for a teenager. However, if the celebrity or fantasy figure becomes the child's confidante, their closest friend, offering greater safety than the adult world, then someone needs to step in with a suitable alternative; to encourage the child to join a club, a sport, music, a youth group and so on.

Kirja's Theme
Resilience

Kirja and others like her deserve medals for resilience, for not giving up on life and for creating strategies that help them cope with the unstable reality of their everyday existence. Kirja, as a carer, worries about her father and is obedient to him as he demands food or drink or that she come down to watch TV. Their relationship is ill-defined, as they spend much time in separate rooms, rarely speaking. Kirja does the washing and attends school but without obvious support. Does the school know what her home life is like? What happens to Kirja when her homework is spoilt?

Negatives

- Kirja is lonely, angry, unsupported. How long will this situation continue?

- Kirja's mother convinced herself that the wider world needed her more than her own family. Kirja's strongest connection to her mother is found in the scent bottles. The sense of smell is very powerful and etches itself onto our memory.

- When the community nurse/professional carer visits her father, she neglects to ask him about Kirja and misses a professional opportunity to report possible concerns.

Positives

- Kirja's good nature shines through all the anger and loneliness.

- Kirja's imagination has some positive outcomes, such as being able to pretend that her birthday celebrations are better than they really are.

- Kirja's behaviour is arguably less problematic than other destructive actions such as physical self-harm or substance abuse.

Discussion

- From the story, what obstacles did Kirja have to deal with in her real world?

- When the pressure of life overwhelmed her, Kirja wrecked her room and re-ordered it. How else might a young person deal with this level of stress?

- If you were Kirja's teacher or friend, what would you do for her? Is there any practical advice or action that you could offer that would make a real difference to her life?

Sean
In My Own Words

The Character

Sean is a fifteen year old lad, who lives for the moment. His actions are spontaneous and unpredictable. The story "In My Own Words" is an amalgamation of real events that happened in the lives of several of my pupils. One of them (whose behaviour was extremely erratic) was a very intelligent teenager, good at English language but emotionally confused as the result of a chaotic and violent upbringing. It interested me that a child with very little educational support from home, few if any books and in any case, no parent interested in reading aloud to him, had developed such a wonderful imagination and could produce a sensitive piece of descriptive writing.

As his tutor, it was a challenge to harness this particular boy's flashes of brilliance into a worthwhile academic product.

The real Sean is a competent story-teller who could tell you a colourful story about his own life. Not all the events in the story "In My Own Words" happened to the real Sean. We once fostered a different boy who had suffered many sudden and unexplained house moves and these experiences are mentioned here. This boy's mother never informed schools or doctors, even when moving over a hundred miles, thus the child and his siblings missed vital weeks and months of schooling and social care.

Sean's Theme

Conferring Blame

In the story, Sean blames others for his actions and reactions. He acts without considering the consequences. The list of people in his firing line is varied: mum; absent dad; social workers; aunty Maggs; cousin Sarah; total strangers (such as the people in the court); even his victims (the boys he threatened) who accidentally addressed Sean as YOU. All are blamed by Sean for his predicament.

Negatives

- Sean experienced shifting relationships between parent figures.

- House moves meant uncertainty in education, friendships lost.

- No moral examples or guidance from family / no boundaries.

- Sean's identity was undermined and undervalued from birth onwards.

- Sean shows signs of repeating learnt behaviour when he belittles others, mocks strangers, and distains anyone he doesn't understand.

Positives

- Some professionals involved in his life give Sean positive reinforcement when he does well. They are consistent with him, even when he fails.

- Sean has a quick mind with a good imagination. He is a keen observer of those around him.

- Sean's tutor uses maths and other subjects to teach him about life. Academic ideas dovetail with guidance, so for example; using rods and magnets, Sean understands that a person needs a strong 'internal structure'.

Discussion

- Drugs are not mentioned in this story but how much might you assume 'weed' contributes to Sean's erratic behaviour?

- Is Sean correct in blaming others for his actions?

- Could Sean ever fit into a mainstream school?

- Do you think it is too late to help Sean change his attitude to life?

- At what point in his life, if any, do you think professionals could have helped Sean effectively?

- Sean fantasises that Jack is his real dad. Why? How did Jack maintain the professional boundaries between himself and Sean?

Hetty Who Cares

The Character

Hetty is based on a girl I once knew. In her excellent mainstream school she was placed in the middle ability form but skived on a regular basis, narrowly avoiding exclusion in year 11. She was talented at design and good at fashion. She was and still is articulate and fun-loving, the daughter of caring parents. However, she had a low self-esteem and lacked a clear sense of danger, occasionally finding herself on the wrong side of town in the middle of the night.

The crowd of kids hiding behind the changing rooms on the park was a real event. I know this because I am the woman who confronted them and the conversations and ensuing scenes (apart from the kidnap incident with Hetty), are real. In real life, Hetty was interested in spiritual things and I combined this idea with one of my own memories when I hitch-hiked as a teenager. My penfriend and I accepted a lift in someone's car in the middle of the night. I was in the back dozing, when

I thought I heard a voice say 'pray.' I sat bolt upright and stayed alert the whole journey. It turned out that the man who picked us up was dangerous, but we managed to get away when we arrived in London very early in the morning. Like many young people we never reported the incident to the police. After all, nothing really happened… did it?

Hetty's Theme
Low Self-esteem

In the story and in real life, Hetty's parents are happily married with other children. They genuinely love their daughter and want the best for her, yet somehow, communications have broken down between them and Hetty drifts and dreams through her early teen years. She is easily bored, undervalues her own abilities and sees no reason to try to succeed at school. She has developed the impression that because she is not an A or A* for everything she is therefore no good at anything. Unlike many of her peers for whom perfect makeup and designer gear is paramount, Hetty is careless with her appearance, applying slap-dash makeup and dragging ladders on her tights.

Negatives

- Hetty has developed a bad attitude at home. She has been allowed to dictate the relationship with her parents as she slams doors and never says hello or goodbye. She has become used to doing what she likes when she likes.

- Hetty (and her brother Simon) have not yet developed a sense of empathy for others. Out of sight is out of mind. Hetty doesn't consider others and she does not realise how her choices affect other people at school and at home.

- It takes a very traumatic event to jolt Hetty into realising that other people care about her.

- Hetty is easily led. She is not a leader. She is influenced by her peers who choose to skive, although she harbours a suppressed sense of regret about this.

Positives

- Hetty is not low ability. If she had applied herself to education she could have been in the top set. With guidance she might find work or complete a college art foundation course.

- She has two loving parents.

Discussion

- What could Hetty's parents have done to help her develop a sense of worth?

- What strategies could the school use to help Hetty rather than excluding her?

- Does Hetty's story illustrate 'normal' teenage behaviour?

- Certain behaviour, such as belligerence, laziness or selfishness, is deemed by some to be 'normal' teenage behaviour. Should this be ignored or addressed by parents and teachers?

Oby
Oby and the O

The Character

At only ten years old Oby is the youngest character in this set of stories. He has a quick mind, and like most children he uses wit and imagination to get through one day at a time. He struggles with reading. Oby has probably been placed in the bottom set. He obviously gets away with proverbial murder by bribing his sister and school friends to help with writing tasks. Home life is challenging, so any amount of shouting or timeout is not going to change Oby's ability to cope with school.

Oby's Theme
Illiteracy

The idea for this story came from a foster child of ours who could read well, but at school, if he was asked to do a task that he did not fully understand he would immediately react with some level of violence. He would argue with a tutor or throw a chair. He would invariably be sent to the headteacher who had little patience with the boy. He would be excluded for a week or two then reintroduced to face the same problem. I discovered that his comprehension of the world was confused so I tried to give him the space to ask questions that a three year old might ask, the who, where and why of the world. He felt safe to do this because I did not laugh at him for 'being thick'. The story of Oby is an observation, not a solution.

Negatives

- The lack of understanding of the headteacher – yes he is a caricature, but his emotional distance from the pupil and his personal ambitions are traits I have occasionally witnessed. It goes without saying (but I shall say it anyway) that most of the head teachers I know are exemplary towards their pupils!

- Oby uses avoidance strategies so that he doesn't have to face a written task, but the head also avoids dealing with the real issues in Oby's life by reverting to lies ("I phoned your parents") and prioritising the inspector's visit before properly dealing with the pupil.

Positives

- Oby's imagination is wonderful! Perhaps influenced by TV or internet games or even illustrations in books. Oby not only invents a single world, but a series of worlds to which he can escape. Some of the worlds are more dangerous than the real situation in which Oby finds himself. This idea was inspired by one of my oldest pupils (over sixteen years of age) who had invented an intricate series of worlds in outer space. He named all the new planets, designed transport and intricate plans for moving between planets. He named hundreds of characters and gave them roles and relationships. He did all this in words and pictures as well as building huge spaceships with Lego. He was happiest when being the creator, in control of his own universe.

- Oby is an optimist and makes himself into a winner as he makes the right choice of O.

Discussion

- Can you think of incidents in your school or environment when a child (or even an adult) has 'kicked off' in order to divert attention from the real problem?

- Assuming Oby is receiving support from a SENCO, what else could be done to support him and prevent the inevitable disruption to the mainstream class in future?

- Imagine you are a year nine pupil. Oby is in your class. How could you make school life more manageable for him?

Rosa
Between Two Worlds

The Character

Rosa could be described as a 'hard to place' foster child. She is now with a family who want to care for her, but Rosa cannot trust their love or commitment. Like a crab that moves from shell to shell, Rosa has moved six times and each time hopes that her growing body and developing personality will fit into the new shell perfectly. Rosa might have moved physically to a new environment, but emotionally she has learnt to keep her old shell; to harden it; to squeeze herself into it; to refuse to move on. She refuses to adjust to her new family, because she doesn't feel safe. The new family are loving, caring and determined to cope long term, but Rosa tests them constantly. She is feisty, over-confident but not as streetwise as she thinks.

Rosa is another teenager who lacks a sense of danger. She makes decisions with no consideration of the consequences. Rosa's behaviour as described in this story is based on the real behaviour of two separate fostered children.

Rosa's Theme
Attachment Disorder

Attachment is the deep and lasting bond between a child and its carer. It is formed during the first few years of the child's life and profoundly affects the child's development and ability to express emotions and develop relationships. It is exhausting for a parent who desires to connect with that child. The child might react with defiance or indifference. It may be possible to treat this problem with an abundance of time, patience and love.

A child with an attachment disorder will harbour anger and feels alone. The problem can be the result of repeated negative life experiences, such as neglect, isolation and lack of communication. A crying baby that is never comforted will learn that there is no point in crying. A child that needs food or water or a nappy change becomes confused because sometimes the needs are met but not at other times. The cause might be no one's fault – such as a child needing hospitalisation or being moved through families in the foster care system.

Some of the signs of attachment disorder that Rosa displays are an inability to connect emotionally to her foster parents; she reveals her anger when she writes on her window; if she makes eye contact it is often aggressive; she doesn't seem to care that she spends hours alone in her room.

Negatives

- Rosa makes inappropriate contact with strangers.

- Rosa goes beyond safe boundaries without thinking of the consequences for others.

- Rosa dreams that her birth mother praises her inappropriate actions and encourages her to rebel against the system of care. Rosa wants to believe that she was unjustly removed from her mother by social services.

Positives

- Rosa realises her foster parents did not reject her.

- The team around the child worked well together to resolve the situation.

Discussion

- Can you identify which professionals worked together to support Rosa?

- There are other professionals who could get involved, for example to counsel the child. Who might these be?

- If Rosa was in your class at school, how could you befriend or support her? Or do you think it would be too hard to relate to such an angry, erratic child?

 # Pia
The Broken Compass

The Character

Pia (pronounced PEER – but it really doesn't matter). I wanted to choose a rare name for this child because her situation is hopefully, quite rare. Pia is of average academic ability and has done well enough in a small school designed for children with behavioural difficulties. She lives with her mother, who is barely able to care for Pia. Pia has learnt to be self-sufficient and strong willed. She has demanded a move to mainstream school and is deemed ready to give it a go.

This story is based on the experience of a pupil of mine whose first day of mainstream school was in year ten. She attended a specialist school for children with behavioural difficulties and apparently persuaded staff that she was ready to move to a local secondary school. Some bridging work was done, as the pupil visited the school with her support worker on several occasions. This pupil lasted three weeks before she gave up and stopped attending. She had realised how difficult it was to make friendships so late in the day, as well as coping with the comparatively large numbers of pupils, the rules and the uniform. After a few months without schooling, I became her home tutor.

This pupil was so afraid of what people thought of her that she refused to go to public places without spending literally hours applying fake tan, thick eye makeup and even getting hair extensions. She did not believe she needed help or education and did not want to think about the future.

Pia's Theme
Self-sufficiency

For many children self-sufficiency is a very positive characteristic. An only child might develop a strong sense of coping with life and will become a very capable adult. However in Pia's case she has had to sink or swim. Lack of strong parenting means Pia has had to learn to cope alone. Her determination to attend secondary school and shake off all adult school support could be construed as a positive characteristic. Pia believes that she is just like all the other children who attend the local secondary school, but she has no idea of the reality. She doesn't comprehend the unspoken rules of her peers, such as the way makeup should be applied or not applied or how to relate to teachers or other authority figures. She has no way of knowing the subtleties of human behaviour that enable a person to be accepted into the pack.

Pia does not allow the adult world to influence her life. She dreams only of being accepted as part of a gang or peer group. When, after only a few hours in mainstream school she does not gain social acceptance, Pia impetuously leaves the building and goes home.

Pia shrugs off the failure of her school experience as just another day. She is like a bad car driver, who doesn't realise that all the accidents behind her are caused by her poor driving.

But who taught Pia to drive?

Negatives

- Pia's relationship with her school link worker is weak and the bridging plan wasn't secure.

- Pia is secretive about her home-life and her habits, such as how long it takes her to apply makeup that she relies on to mask her real self.

- Attending mainstream school was highly unlikely to have a successful outcome in the long run.

- Pia floundered in class, with limited comprehension of educational vocabulary. I remember being at school in the 1970s and studying a subject called 'Current Affairs'. I had no idea what the title of this subject meant until I became an adult and saw 'Current Affairs' as a heading in the newspaper! A speaker hasn't really communicated properly until the hearer has total comprehension of the meaning. Teachers must not tire of communicating. And if a pupil doesn't understand the first time...?

Positives

- Mainstream IS an option for some children from specialist units but bridging needs to be very secure. (In reality, financial restraints do not allow for this in many instances).

- Pia did manage to attend school independently, despite her support worker being late.

Discussion

- "I have already taught you that!" says the exasperated teacher. If we become sick and tired of communicating we may be failing in our job, so how can we find fresh, creative ways to ensure our pupil/listener finally understands the point. Is this asking too much or being too idealistic?

- How do you feel about going into a new place with new people? Think about schools, churches, conferences, youth group or other places? What makes this experience easier or more manageable? What would make you want to run a mile from this place? (Think about feeling disorientated, being a stranger in a crowd, unspoken rules that others seem to understand, someone speaking to you and being too friendly/unfriendly).

- Realistically a mainstream teacher does not have enough time to communicate at every level with every pupil. Is this true?

- What circumstances might force a child into becoming too independent too young? In what ways can this be a positive thing? (I'm thinking Richard

Branson here! Find out how young he was when his mum started to train him in adventure!).

- Pia's issue has been described as self-sufficient. What can we learn from Pia's attitude to life?

Blake
Diamondman

The Character

Diamondman is a fictional story, loosely based on several events in the life of one of my pupils. Names and some details are changed to protect identities.

The real 'Blake' had experienced a traumatic upbringing. His mum had several younger children and smoked pot. Her relationships were erratic and Blake was never sure who his real dad was. His real dad was in prison for GBH (Grievous Bodily Harm). Blake had witnessed his dad being cruel to his mother as well as using hard drugs. Blake was never disciplined unless he got in the way of the adults in the house, then 'discipline' was often extreme, violent, and loud. When Blake stayed out on the streets, even as a primary child, he was never reported missing by his mum.

In spite of all this, he was and probably still is a very intelligent boy. He was fascinated by outer space. This interest was sparked by a laminated poster pinned to the wall of his care home. It showed the primary planets and described them in some detail. Blake read and re-read this and learnt many of the facts. He was encouraged to research planets and stars on the computer and became particularly fascinated by Jupiter. One day, as part of an English project, this pupil composed his own version of Diamondman.

Blake had learnt violence and could be violent. He was easily bored and his behaviour became increasingly erratic. He could scale the exterior walls of the care home and sit on the roof, mocking pedestrians. He had also received ASBOs for attacks on young people.

Many people tried to support him, from youth offender services, substance abuse advisors, tutors, care home managers, medics and the police. I can't say that anyone succeeded. I can't tell you the outcome of his life because Blake is still making life choices and some of those will be bad choices.

Diamondman was written to highlight the intelligence of some of these so called 'hoodie boys'. In no way do I condone criminal behaviour, nor do I sympathise in any way with offenders, but neither should a young person be labelled with emotive journalistic language that is unconstructive and potentially damaging. (Examples? Yob; monster; evil thug; and so on).

I believe it is normal for many teens to experience some level of confusion between fantasy and reality. Fantasy is one means of coping with tough situations. I once taught a year 7 girl whose dream was to live in a castle with a prince. She had been neglected and abused as a toddler, fostered in several families and then adopted by parents who struggled to feel emotions towards her. A fantasist might place unrealistic expectations on others, imagining them to be a rescuer or saviour figure, a knight in shining armour.

In 'Diamondman,' Blake creates a fantasy companion (Peter Tanner) to share his adventure. Peter is the one who dies, leaving Blake as the ultimate survivor. The hero mentality means that Blake feels indestructible, even in court. In real life he develops a swagger, believing no one can touch him, no one can hurt him or punish him for his actions.

In Diamondman, the voices of adults are mostly incomprehensible to the teenager who is unused to logical conversation unlaced with swear words. Yes,

Blake does understand the court system, more clearly than you or I and he might even revel in the attention it offers. The court places certain expectations upon him, to turn up on time, to affirm his real identity and to accept responsibility for his actions.

These adults rightly give attention to the Blakes of this world who do wrong. Would the same adults show this much interest if they did everything right?

Yes, Blake was difficult. He had had a complicated life. He needed to know who his real dad was. He wanted his own blood family to be proud of him for something, anything, but in reality he could never make that happen.

Blake's Theme
Unfulfilled Intelligence

Intelligence is the product of nature and nurture. It can also be taught and improved. Intelligence can be intellectual, artistic, musical, emotional and spiritual. It can be masked or destroyed by substance abuse, violence and neglect of a person.

In Diamondman, Blake's intelligence is revealed in many ways; his natural interest in a subject, his ability to absorb information, his imaginative creativity and so on. The question is; if Blake had been more privileged, born or adopted into a caring family, would he have made better life choices? Would he have excelled at school?

The story reveals Blake's kind of logic, his own blend of consciousness of the space where the real and imaginary world meet.

Negatives

- Blake faces court without his family.

- Blake is so immersed in fantasy that he is unlikely to accept the reality of his situation.

- Blake is so used to the 'system' that he has become cocky and believes he is untouchable. It is a total shock for Blake to be served with a six month detention. Previous court disciplines such as ASBOs and curfews had not sufficiently affected Blake to help him change his life for the better.

Positives

- There is good professional support around the child.

- Blake has to face reality when he receives six months detention for his crime.

Discussion

- *"She doesn't even know me."* Blake hears a 'posh woman' trying to defend him by highlighting his social and educational deficiencies. She minimises Blake's abilities and intelligence in order to gain the court's pity. Can this woman really be expected to 'know' her client?

- Who else mocked Blake for showing an interest in 'space study?' This person was sarcastic towards Blake. Blake is not someone we are meant to approve of. He presents as obnoxious, cocky and difficult to relate to. In what way does a sarcastic response help Blake? Can you think of a more appropriate and practical response?

- Is a poor background a valid defence for criminal behaviour?

- "When I grow up I want to be an astronaut." Blake said this when he was young but claims no one believed him. How might a teacher have tapped into this early insight into Blake's mind? (I once taught a boy from a farming background. He was in the lowest set of year 8. He only showed genuine interest when the subject matter was tractors or dogs, so whenever it was possible I included tractors or dogs in the subject matter. At least he produced *some* work!).

- Diamondman is Blake's creation. He will never receive an academic grade for this imaginative story. Is there a danger that we rely too heavily on academic outcomes in order to assess a person? Or is levelling and grading an essential tool for evaluating a pupil accurately?

- Is there anything you could praise Blake for?

- If you met Blake in real life, how would you react to him?

A Last Word from the Author
Why Bother With These Kids?

A simple, true story.

I knock at the door of the terraced house, but no one answers. The sickly aroma of weed wafts through the ill-fitting window. I look up. A bedroom curtain flicks. A shadow moves. I knock again, very loudly, not so polite this time. Then I call his name.

"Dane! Hello, Dane?" I knock gently at the front window. I wait twenty minutes. Yes, twenty whole minutes. Now, I knock firmly on the window and at last I hear footsteps. I step back. Wait.

Click. The door opens on its chain. The tired eyes of a woman blink at the light behind me.

"Yes?" she says, as if she has just woken up. It is midday.

"Hello! Do you remember me from last week? I'm Dane's new tutor. You signed the contract and I gave you his timetable. Is he in?"

"He doesn't want to go with you."

"Does he know I'm here?"

"No."

"But I think he does. Is that his room above us?" I smile, reassuring.

"Yes. But he never goes out."

"Please fetch him downstairs so at least we can meet." I nod enthusiastically as the door shuts in my face.

"Dane!" the woman screams, not bothering to ascend the stairs to speak to her son and a man yells at her to shut the hell up. Dane's mum shouts through the door at me.

"He says no! Try again next week." I wait five minutes. I check my watch. Wait. Knock again. Knock again. Suddenly the door opens. It is Dane, fifteen years old, skinny, pale, spotty, bad teeth.

"Hi," he mumbles shyly.

"Good to meet you Dane!" I smile without embarrassing him by offering to shake hands.

"Are you ready to go?" I glance at Dane's bare feet sticking out white beneath his grey tracksuit. I allow him a few seconds to assess me; after all we are both strangers.

"It's okay," I say, "No reading or writing today. Let's just have a drink in Sainsbury's. You can tell me what you want out of life."

Dane shuts the door in my face. Five minutes later it opens and Dane emerges wearing trainers. He doesn't have the aggressive attitude of his mum, or of most of my other pupils. He sits quietly in my car. I discover it is the first time he has spoken to a teacher of any sort in almost two years.

"How can that happen in this day and age?" you ask. I can't tell you the full story because I must keep the confidence of the school that Dane attended so long ago, and then 'forgot' to attend. Apparently a staff member assumed he had moved away. The school did try to check up on him, but Dane's parents never answered the phone. Then a change in school leadership meant that Dane fell through the net. The day Dane didn't bother with school turned into a month, into a year, into a habit. Into silence.

Dane's parents were otherwise occupied with their own problems.

One day a primary school head requested that Social Services investigate the home life of his much younger sister and at last someone realised Dane was alone upstairs, playing on an X-Box.

After our first meeting, Dane rarely missed a tutorial session. I was only employed to teach him for six hours per week. It's expensive and money doesn't grow on trees. For our first full lesson we visited the National Football Museum (since sadly closed) and afterwards I asked Dane, "So what did you learn?" expecting him to say something about footie and he replied,

"I learnt that I like history more than football." So we repeatedly went back as Dane learnt to read the signs on the doors and to ask endless questions about everything from Queen Victoria to Elvis or the World Wars.

Other times we studied in Sainsbury's café where Dane usually knocked back a pint of milk with a banana! He had never ventured beyond Preston so we went on a 'school trip' to Blackpool Zoo. Even the short motorway drive was an adventure to Dane.

Dane could read very little, his comprehension was minimal and he could not write at all. His hand shook with fear and tension when I handed him a pen. He cried when a woman from Young People's Services asked him to fill in a form. She insisted that he complete it himself and she was right to encourage the independence. Dane quivered and his pale face blotched red and white.

"Sorry," I told the woman, "We'll have to leave it here. Can we try again another day?" She left and I tried to rebuild Dane's confidence.

"It won't be too long and you'll be able to write your full name and address!" I said. "Don't give up at the first hurdle."

A year later, Dane decided to join the army which is a brilliant plan for someone who needs a steady family; although initially I doubted that he would have the mental and physical capacity to succeed. We practiced the army BARB test online. He did well. Oh, the surprise and joy on his face when he passed the English challenge! At my request, Social Services kindly provided Dane with new trainers so we could time him running the required mile and a half.

The army application demanded a birth certificate which Dane's mum failed to produce. She refused to pay the £9 for it, making excuses for not having the money right now. Social Services were brilliant and provided the necessary fee and assured me they would certainly recoup this from Dane's mum. Together Dane and I visited the Lancashire Certificate Service by the Preston docks. The man behind the glass produced a terrifying but straightforward form for him to fill in.

I was amazed when Dane sat at the desk and carefully, painstakingly completed the form himself. A year earlier he would not have had the courage to enter the building, let alone to speak to a stranger or to hold a pen while being watched by anyone other than myself. He handed his form to the clerk who told us to return in an hour.

We walked around the docks and I pointed out words which seemed to leap out at us; warning notices about the dangers of water; instructions on lifebelts; names of boats; stickers in car windows; most of which Dane read aloud hesitantly. We talked about life issues, bullying, temptations, possibilities, hope; until our time was up.

Back at LCS, Dane approached the official. I hovered in the background, more nervous than he was. Dane mumbled confidently (yes that is possible for a teenage boy!) and asked the stranger for his brand new birth certificate.

Five minutes later we sat in my car. Dane grinned as he realised the enormity of his achievement.

"I filled that form in myself," he announced, as if I hadn't noticed, "and now I've got my own birth certificate that tells me about my real dad. I'm going to show this to the army man in town." Then out of the blue, Dane added seven wonderful words;

"I feel like a real man now!"

And it's true.

If a man can read and write he can walk tall.

Note: Names (including Dane's) and and some events in this book have been changed to protect identities.

Biography

Katharine Angel was born in Beckenham in Kent in 1959. Her father Robert joined the RAMC, so the family moved many times and Katharine's primary years were mostly spent in Singapore, Malaysia and Germany. Secondary education was in Bath, then Cornwall and, after a summer of hitching round Europe, she ended up in London where she trained as a teacher. She has taught 'many subjects to all ages of pupil,' in a hotchpotch of schools. Until recently she worked with the National Teaching and Advisory Service which specialises in inclusion for those pupils who have been permanently excluded from education. She and her family have had the privilege of fostering many children over the years.

During 2012 Katharine will be a visiting lecturer in PSHCE for teacher trainers at Edge Hill University.

Katharine has written two series of stories especially for teens who 'need to succeed to read,' to encourage them to enjoy reading for its own sake. In 1987 Katharine was first runner-up in a Lion/ Strait short story competition with the daunting theme of the battle between good and evil in the universe! She wrote '*The Lives of Stanley Pritchard*,' described by some as '*an early version of Sliding Doors*,' which you can read for free on *katharineangel.yolasite.com*

And like all writers, she is working on *that* novel!

Lightning Source UK Ltd.
Milton Keynes UK
UKOW01f0513190716

278706UK00001B/26/P